Frowning, Summer shut off the drying unit.

He stepped clear of it, listening.

There came the noise again. Something scratching on the outside door of his cabin.

Putting on a terrirobe, he left the bathroom to cross to the door of the compartment.

A clawed hand was apparently scraping at the neowood paneling.

After taking the stungun from his robe pocket, he eased the door open.

Ezra Zilber was out in the corridor. His fur was standing on end, his staring eyes had a milky cast and his raised right arm was contorted. "Terribly . . . important . . ."

"Was just going to come looking for you," said Summer. "What the hell's wrong with you?"

Berkley books by Ron Goulart

AFTER THINGS FELL APART

GALAXY JANE

SUICIDE, INC.

BATTLESTAR GALACTICA 8: GREETINGS FROM EARTH
(with Glen A. Larson)

BATTLESTAR GALACTICA 9: EXPERIMENT IN TERRA
(with Glen A. Larson)

BATTLESTAR GALACTICA 10: THE LONG PATROL
(with Glen A. Larson)

RON GOULART

GALAXY JANE

BERKLEY BOOKS, NEW YORK

GALAXY JANE

A Berkley Book/published by arrangement with
the author

PRINTING HISTORY
Berkley edition/March 1986

Cover art by Boris Vallejo.

For information address: The Berkley Publishing Group,
200 Madison Avenue, New York, New York 10016.

ISBN: 0-425-08684-4

A BERKLEY BOOK ® TM 757,375

PRINTED IN THE UNITED STATES OF AMERICA

GALAXY JANE

1

The three glittering robots who attacked him on the ground level of the shuttleport were only three feet high but full of nasty tricks.

Jack Summer, a middle-sized sandy-haired man of thirty-nine, had been striding toward the glaz doors leading to the NewzNet takeoff area, when a certain amount of whooping and hollering commenced behind him.

"There's the blighter!"

"That's him! Summer the philanderer!"

"Let's us give 'im what-for!"

Spinning around, Summer found himself facing a trio of midget robots. There were sneers and scowls showing on their silvery ballheads, the words *Scoundrel Trackers, Ltd.* engraved in gloletters on their metallic chests.

"Fellas," said Summer, grinning amiably and holding up a hand in a stop-right-there gesture, "I think I know who's hired you and—"

"Dirty sod!"

"Irresponsible lout!"

"Bloody wretch!"

One of them leaped, tackling Summer just below the

knees, causing him to fall over backward. He landed on the plaz mosaic tiles with a slick thump.

A second Scoundrel Trackers robot jumped and sat, hard, on Summer's chest. "Now give a listen to this, mate." Music started pouring out of a tiny speaker in his left side. Sweet, romantic music thick with violins.

"So?" Summer got an armlock on the squatting robot and tried to unseat him.

"Ain't 'e the 'eartless one?" observed the third robot, who'd opened a compartment in his shiny chest to reveal a small wafer-thin vidscreen.

"This here's *your* song," said the one on Summer's chest. "The very tune you and your dear wife loved to play of an evening whilst gathered round the bloomin' 'armonium in—"

"You gents do sloppy research," Summer pointed out while trying to wrestle free of the two mechanical men. "Maryella and I never owned a harmonium. Furthermore, that dippy tune is actually the theme from an old Galactic Skymines commercial that aired here in the Barnum System of planets nearly five long—"

"An' I suppose, you cruel deserter," inquired the third robot, tapping his picture screen, "that this hain't that selfsame Maryella workin' as a galley drudge in a cafeteria what's orbitin' the worst bloomin' planet out in the Hellquad at this—"

"Nope, it isn't," said Summer after a quick glance at the flickering image. "Maryella's slim and blond, thirty-one her last birthday. That lady's got to be over fifty and she's fat as well, and—"

"Well, the poor lass 'as gone to seed since you run off to pursue your dubious career as a muckrakin' video-journalist, guv."

"I didn't run off. Maryella and I are legally divorced." He managed to toss the robot from off his chest, sending it smack into the one who was showing him the heartrending pictures of a woman who wasn't his former wife at all.

Both of the 'bots went rolling and sliding, wobbling and rattling, away from him.

That left only the third mechanical billcollector, who had both springy metal arms locked around Summer's legs.

"I suppose," asked this one now in his tinny, piping voice, "you're goin' to claim you don't owe the poor slatternly wench four bloody months of back alimony?"

"That was just an error on the part of my bank. While I was out on the planet—"

"Can the tripe, guv. All you deadbeats try to pull that . . . Awk! Awk!"

Summer thrust a hand into the mechanical man's right armpit, locating the emergency turnoff switch. Few knew of the switch, but Summer'd done considerable research on bizbots once, for a seven-minute vidwall essay that never aired.

Jumping to his feet and clear of the disabled 'bot, he went sprinting for the NewzNet gates.

The other two Scoundrel Trackers, Ltd. mechanical men were still struggling to return to upright positions.

The large toadman paused to fluff his curly golden locks, then continued, "What you don't seem to understand, young man, is that this—"

"I'm not young," corrected Summer, who was seated across the shuttle aisle from the toad in the conservative two-piece bizsuit.

"Be that as it may, this is, as is plainly spelled out on the cabin door, in not one but seventeen major languages and a rebus, this is an Executive Shuttle to the NewzNet satellite headquarters."

"Yep, that's exactly where I want to go." Nodding, Summer settled back in his plush seat.

The shuttle was climbing silently up toward Studio One, his intended destination.

"The point is," persisted the toadman with an angry

toss of his curls, "you aren't an executive, do you see? You're merely a field reporter—and one noted for his flippancy, his padded expense accounts, his notorious tendency to seduce every and all—"

"Yes, he's got disgusting morals," put in a hefty humanoid lady of sixty-one who was sitting a few seats ahead.

"Good morning, Henrietta," said Summer with a grin. "You're looking svelte."

"I am not, Summer. I'm looking fat and gross as usual," said Henrietta Dorf, frowning back at him over her broad shoulder. "Don't try any of that dreadful blarney you work on barmaids, hookers, floozies, skin models, tarts—"

"Henrietta," interrupted Summer, "in the nearly eleven months that I've been working for NewzNet, my life in the field has been one of exemplary conduct, spotless morality and—"

"Grout puckey," observed Henrietta, jiggling disdainfully. "You forget, Summer, that I'm a Vice President in our Legal Department. All the complaints that pour in about your wretched conduct cross my desk. Why, even your poor frail ex-wife, who's been forced to work as a hostess in an animal shelter orbiting one of the meanest planets in the Trinidad System out—"

"Maryella lives in a villa on Esmeralda," said Summer. "It's just that her attorneys, especially the android one, are fairly imaginative. They cook up various false yarns whenever I happen, due to glitches on the part of my bank, to fall a week or two behind in my alimony pay—"

"There's another terrible thing," said the glowering lady exec. "You go around from planet to planet doing reports about the faults and failings of others, while you owe that poor girl a stewpot of dough and she—"

"Hoy!" boomed someone from up at the front of the shuttle cabin. "Give Jack a break, huh? He's one hell of an investigative reporter, always has been." A big, wide catman stood up to face the other three passengers on this NewzNet Executive Shuttle. He was wearing a one-piece paramilitary worksuit, and had a patch over his right eye.

"Wink Bowman," said Summer. "I didn't notice you slouched up there."

Bowman came lumbering up the aisle. "Now, I happen to be the best damn war correspondent NewzNet's got," he admitted. "But Jack here's the best muckraker, the absolute top man at digging out all the sordid details of political scandals, criminal intrigues and dubious flimflams of all sorts. I remember when he was working in the print medium . . . *Muckrake Magazine*, wasn't it? He used to travel to the hotest hot spots and the worst pestholes in our Barnum System. He worked with a horny photog name of . . . LaPenna, wasn't it?"

"Palma," said Summer.

"Palma, yeah, that was the guy's name. Baldest and horniest chap I've ever run into." The burly catman chuckled. "I remember one time on Murdstone when they found Palma, snerg naked, in the Sacred Convent of Our Lady of the Wobbly Knees just as the Streamlined Bishop arrived to bless the—"

"Wink," interrupted Henrietta, "I know all these vile tales already, they fill to fat Jack Summer's file. There's really no need to repeat them."

The toadman cleared his throat. "It certainly sounds to me as though this fellow isn't NewzNet material at all," he said. "We stand, let me remind you, for a certain moral and—"

"Listen, Virgil," said the war correspondent, pointing a furry finger at him, "Summer's last three reports for us were picked up by more vidwall stations across the universe than anything else NewzNet's done this year. The gross income from his—"

"There's no need," put in Henrietta, "to babble confidential information in front of—"

"I hadn't heard about those sales figures, Wink." Summer invited him to sit beside him. "Can you give me more details?"

The catman eased down next to him. "Thinking of asking for a pay hike?"

"I'm almost always thinking about that," admitted Summer.

2

His small green editor made one more slow circuit of the glazwalled office. "Well, sir, I might be able to get you an additional 50,000 trudollars," he said slowly. "Not much more."

"That'll help a little."

"I understand your poor wife has been forced to take employment as a groutherder on a pastoral space colony that orbits—"

"Ex-wife," corrected Summer, who was sitting on a rubberoid sofa and gazing down through the vufloor at the planet Barnum below them. "Yes, it's sad what lack of money will lead you to, Fred."

Carefully Fred Taliaferro made his way back to his lucite desk. "For a while I thought I might get over my fear of heights," he said, not looking down. "No such luck."

Summer suggested, "Have your floor and walls opaqued."

The green man hopped into his desk chair. "Nope, that'd make them think I was flawed," he said as he picked up a pile of faxsheets of various sizes and colors. "Well, sir, let's get down to . . . um . . . by the way, did you insult Virgil Brigmush?"

"Might have. Who is he?"

"Senior VP in Marketing. Claims you took an unauthorized ride up here this morning, were rude to him and used gutter language.

Grinning, Summer nodded. "I did all that, except for the foulmouth stuff."

"Jack, I keep trying to explain to you that, while NewzNet is the most liberal news and reporting service in this corner of the universe, the management people tend—"

"I'll control my impulses next time. Some robots were chasing me around the port down there, so I caught the first shuttle for here that—"

"Have you ever sat down with a computer and drawn up a budget? That way you wouldn't be dunned all the—"

"The new assignment," reminded Summer.

"Hum?" Blinking twice, Taliaferro glanced at the papers he was holding in his bright green hands. "Yes, right. You know about the illegal drug called Zombium?"

"Sure, nasty stuff. Most of it comes from the back country on the planet Murdstone. I did a piece on the Zombium traffic for *Muckrake* six or seven years—"

"I read it, yes." His editor fluttered the handful of papers. "Maybe, you know, you ought not to talk openly about how long ago you wrote for that magazine, Jack. This is a young man's business, afterall. At least the field reporter end of it. The fact you're nearly thirty-five might—"

"I'll be forty in January."

Taliaferro gave a forlorn shake of his head. "That's even worse. Well, sir, you don't look that old, so maybe—"

"Let's get back to the Zombium story. Does NewzNet want me to travel out to Murdstone to—"

"Yes, but not directly." Taliaferro plucked a yellow sheet from his fistful. "We've been getting rumors . . . fairly reliable ones . . . that a spacecraft known as *Hollywood II* may be involved in smuggling the stuff."

Summer said, "That's one of those vidmovie outfits, roams the Barnum System making flix. Yep, they'd be in a position to smuggle most anything. Who's the source of your rumors?"

His green editor didn't meet his eyes. "He'd prefer not to be involved any furth—"

"C'mon, Fred, I don't work that way."

"Okay, all right. I'll supply you with the name, but don't contact him directly unless—"

"You want me to go onboard the *Hollywood II*?"

"Exactly, yes." Taliaferro held up another sheet of paper, salmon-colored this time. "You'll be pretending to do a story on their latest production. It's entitled . . . where is that memo? Yes, *Galaxy Jane*."

"Galaxy Jane was a space pirate in this system back ninety years ago or so."

"Yes, so it says here. She had a lair on Murdstone and was also involved in some native uprisings," said the editor. "Apparently the movie's going to concentrate on that phase of her colorful career."

"Convenient for them if they are smuggling Zombium," observed Summer. "The weed the stuff's concocted from grows all over the Pegada Territory, which is also where Galaxy Jane operated in her heyday."

Taliaferro selected a purplish sheet of faxpaper, scanned it, frowned, let it drop to one side. "We'll want you to interview the stars of this opus. Let me see . . . Francis X. Yoe will be portraying . . . um . . . Captain Thatcher King of the Royal Mounted Stungunners and

. . . I wish the printer down in Backgrounding didn't have this fuzzy sanserif typeface . . . Yes, this says Flo Haypenny is going to be Galaxy Jane."

Summer looked again at his editor. "She's a onetime Zombium user."

"I didn't know that. But then I was in Sports for three years before they stuck me here in Scandal and Crime and so I—"

"Supposedly she was cured after a stay at Greenmansions, that rehab colony out by—"

"When was this?" He was scribbling marginal notes with his electropen.

"Seven years back."

"That long ago? Is Flo Haypenny old, too?"

"Thirty-five."

Taliaferro shook his head. "Sad," he observed. "Well, sir, you're scheduled to board the *Hollywood II* when it docks at Spaceport/A down on Barnum tomorrow afternoon. You'll stay onboard during the two-day jaunt out to Murdstone, hang around while they do location work. We'd like to get something good from you—it has to play at least six minutes—within a week or less."

"May take longer."

"Budget and Allocations gets on my tail if my people drag—"

"I'll give it a valiant try, Fred."

His editor pushed the collection of papers across the desk top. "You can browse through these, then return them to me."

"You forgot a page." Summer nodded at the purple sheet.

"Hum?"

"There."

"Oh, this?" Gingerly he lifted it. "Jack, suppose . . . well, suppose I get you a raise of 75,000 trubux?"

"Who?"

"What?"

"Who do you want me to drag along on this damn assignment with me?"

"You're making it sound like something unpleasant, whereas it might be as much fun as a barrel of—"

"All I need is a cambot to take my footage." Summer stood up. "The way I operate, a partner isn't—"

"The thing is . . . Well, sir, this directive isn't from me." He pointed a green finger upward. "Comes from higher."

"Who are you burdening me with?"

"They tell me . . . reliable sources inform me, since I've never met the lady . . . that she's very . . . hum . . . cute. Bright, too. She graduated with honors from the Barnum School of Visual Arts and Investigative Reporting last autumn."

"Last fall?" Summer leaned, rested his palms on the desk and studied Taliaferro's anxious face. "You're sticking me with a child? Some girl fresh out of a convent? Fred, these Zombium traffickers are tough and dirty."

"Would you care to look at her grades? She got an A– in Dirty Combat, a B+ in Wilderness Survival. So you have nothing to—"

Straightening, Summer took a step back from the lucite desk. "Nugent," he realized. "It's Nugent's daughter, isn't it? That blond tomboy who—"

"Jack, hush. Eli Nugent's the Associate Chairman of the whole damn NewzNet operation," he said in a low, cautious voice. "Sure, Vicky Nugent happens to be his only daughter, but she's supposed to be a crackerjack journalist as well."

"No, nope, not at all." Summer headed for a door. "I'm not going to play nanny to some nitwit heiress who thinks she's—"

"100,000 trubux," called Taliaferro.

Halting, Summer turned to face the desk again. "Put that in writing."

The editor nodded. "I'll draw up an agreement in triplicate," he pledged. "We'll even shake hands on the deal."

Summer narrowed his left eye. "Okay, I'll work with Vicky Nugent."

Taliaferro allowed himself a small relieved smile. "She's supposed to be," he said, "very personable."

3

The three tattooed gatormen who attacked Summer in the Central Foyer of Barnum Spaceport/A the next afternoon were carrying rolled-up parasols.

While the huskiest of the trio, who had an idealized portrait of his mother etched in glowhite on his leathery bicep, dived and attempted to tackle the vidjournalist, the other two started whacking at him with their polka-dot umbrellas.

"Thus to all deadbeats and alimony cheats!" cried the Scoundrel Trackers, Ltd. agent who was whapping Summer on his back and shoulders.

"It pays to pay up on time," suggested the third. He was profusely decorated with tattooed sporting scenes and was making swordsmanlike lunges with his furled parasol.

"Spare me the commercial messages." Summer dodged the thrusts of the umbrella, moving out of the way of a line of scurrying wheeled baggagebots, and got in three good solid jabs to the collection agent's protruding snout.

The gator's massive jaws clacked twice, his eyes rolled back as he proceeded to fold up. He tumbled against a stationary candybot, clutched at it and then sank to the rippled glaz floor.

"Oops, oops!" The copper-plated candybot started making apologetic hooting noises. Plaz-wrapped carob-coated grasshoppers were starting to spout out of a nozzle in its chest.

"The tab is mounting," said the gatorman, who'd succeeded in tackling Summer and was struggling to bring him down. "Four months back alimony to that poor foresaken lady who must toil as a tapdancer in a stage-door canteen orbiting Perennial War Planet Number 22 out in the boonies of the universe. Add to that the cost of massive repairs and mental anguish balm to our three personable pint-sized robots yesterday. And now you've rearranged Otto's schnozzle and broken a servomech—"

"G'wan, your damn insurance covers all that."

"Don't step on those disgusting candied bugs, my children," warned a Streamlined Bishop as he escorted a dozen and a half catkids toward an excursion rocket gate. "Don't become entangled in this loathsome and brutal brawl."

"Are these guys soused to the eyeballs?" inquired a little catgirl in pinafore and sudostraw hat.

"Alas, one fears so." The furry cleric hurried them out of range.

"We'll add that to your bill, too," said the gator. "Tearing down our reputations by associating with you, Summer."

"Hooey," he observed, jumping free of the gatorman's armhold. As he rose in the air, Summer kicked him a good one on the chin.

"Unk." His tattooed assailant went staggering back, crossing the path of a birdpeople honeymoon party before passing out at the foot of a decorative plaz palm tree.

The bride shrieked, yellow and green feathers standing on end. "Oh, I told you this junket was jinxed, Jerome," she said. "We should've settled for that skyvan trip daddy offered to spring for."

"Relax, Martha, relax," soothed her duck-billed husband, urging her around another of the stately palms. "Nothing more than a few nitwits clowning around."

Summer turned to face the Scoundrel Tracker who'd been attacking him from behind. "My Banx branch's taking care of the alimony situation even as we speak," he explained cordially. "Why don't you just gather up your fallen comrades and slink quietly—"

"In a snerg's valise, buddy." This one had intricate pastoral scenes emblazoned on his powerful arms and the large patch of broad chest showing through his low-cut tunic. "Notice the ferrule of this bumbershoot I happen to have aimed right smack at your goonies. Looks a lot like a stungun barrel, don't it now?"

"You try to use a stungun on me, chum, and I'll shut down your whole and entire—"

"Won't use it if you trot along peaceable to our local STL office, which is conveniently located only minutes away from downtown—"

Zzzzzzzummmmmmm!

Summer flinched and dived sideways at the sound of a stungun.

When the third and final billcollector fell over, Summer realized the parasol hadn't been fired at all.

Glancing around, he noticed a slim blond young woman standing next to a pile of space luggage a few yards to his left. She was pretty, not more than twenty-two, clad in a short-skirted two-piece cazsuit. As she smiled tentatively across at him, she tucked a small silver-plated, jewel-handled stungun back into a thigh holster.

The curious little catgirl had strayed from her group and was now perched on a floating plazbench watching the slender blond. "Is this one of those crimes of passion?" she inquired, her straw hat now clutched between her furry little paws.

"Kathryn, come away from this scene of horrible depravity." The Streamlined Bishop snatched her up off the bench, tucked her under one stout arm and went trotting away through the small curious crowd that was building a circle around Summer, the fallen gatormen and the helpful blond.

"I sure hope I haven't offended you or anything, Mr. Summer," she said, taking a few cautious steps in his direction. "What I mean is, you may have some darn masculine code that compels you, I don't know, to handle any and all attackers singlehanded without the least little bit of—"

"Nope, I accept whatever help I can get," he assured her. "So, thanks."

"Hey, and listen. You aren't, are you, chagrined or anything because I overheard all this guff about your darn marital problems and all? What I'm getting at is this: you probably weren't planning to much like me anyway and this on top—"

"You're Vicky Nugent."

Her smile became somewhat less timid and she moved closer. "Matter of fact, I am, yes," she answered, nodding. "See, I got myself here a little early so I could, I don't know, take a look at you before I finally introduced myself. I'm not, as you probably've figured, exactly timid, but when I get a chance to work with a galactically renowned reporter like you, I tend to get—"

"Half a moment, you two. What say we knock off

this old home week crapola and get down to cases?" A burly spacesailor whose tanned face and arms were rich with tattoos of a patriotic nature stepped free of the onlookers to scowl, hands on hips, at Summer and the young woman. "Now, in my book gatormen are the scum of the universe. To me they're only one step above lizardmen, who are known far and wide as the sludge in the booptube of humanity and—"

"Hold it, schmucko," growled a lizard commando in full regalia. "I'm passing through on me way to the 19th Annual Purebred Aryan Lizard Conclave out on the planet Barafunda. Your ethnic slurs don't sit well with me nor—"

"Whyn't you let me speak my entire piece, blockhead," said the spacesailor. "I was about to explain that, while I wouldn't wipe a grout's toke with your average gatorman, I have an affinity for anyone who's had the wisdom to have him or herself tattooed at some juncture in life. Tattooing, if I may wax eloquent about my hobbyhorse for a bit, is a much maligned artform in this benighted corner of the universe. Therefore, anybody what belts not one—" He held up his tattooed fingers as he ticked them off. "Not two—but three handsome walking examples of the tattooists art, I am—"

"Scram," suggested Vicky quietly.

"Whoa now, sister," said the sailor with a scowl. "No beanpole of a bimbo can tell Mr. Spaceshipman Easy to fire his rockets and—"

"Gents," said Summer to the spacesailor and the commando, "unless you want to join this unconscious trio of art specimens, I suggest you cease blabbing and get the hell out of our way."

The lizard man said, "We space commandos, kiddo, don't take orders from middle-sized ginks who—"

"We really don't have any more time to stall around," said Vicky near Summer's left ear. "I've spotted a couple of those darn Port Security cops starting to push their way over here. Let's make a dash for our ship."

"Okay, you start and I'll settle with these two louts."

"No need for that, Mr. Summer. Scoop can handle them."

"Scoop?"

"Scoop/104P-1K. He's my camera robot—well, our camera robot actually," she explained. "Except he's sort of special, customized and all. My father gave me Scoop when I graduated from—"

"All we need is a regular everyday cambot on this—"

"What'd I tell you, angelcake, about teaming up with this superannuated yawp?" A large mechanical man emerged from behind the pyramid of baggage. "He can't even dodder across the port without—"

"Scoop, dear, would you take care of these annoying gentlemen?"

"A snap." The robot was chrome-plated, trimmed with glittering semiprecious stones. His head, based vaguely on that of a handsome humanoid, had a camera lens mounted above his two gleaming ruby eyes.

"What's the flaming big idea?" demanded the irate sailor. "Our squabble is with you two, not this tool of—"

"Couple of snurfheads," observed Scoop as he raised his right hand and pointed a metallic forefinger at the spaceshipman.

Zzzzzittttzzzzzz!

A thin beam of intensely green light jumped from the tip of the robot's extended finger and hit the illustrated forehead of the spacesailor.

He flapped his muscular arms twice, rose up on his toes, made a low yowling noise and then fell over backward into a faxpaper newsie.

"Wuxtry! Wuxtry!" yelped the kid-sized newsbot.

The lizard commando swallowed, tipped his helmet

and said, "Nice meeting you, one and all." He pushed away through the by-standers.

Scoop rubbed at his gleaming chest with the fingers of his right hand. "What say, sugarbunch, we leave this antiquated newzhound here and catch the—"

"Now you can escort us to the *Hollywood II* docking area," requested Vicky, "before yonder cops reach us."

The robot's disappointed sigh rattled various components within him. "Here you've got one of the journalistic lights of the whole snurfheaded universe working for you and you prefer Summer, who's been obsolete since—"

"Scoop. Now."

After letting a smaller sigh escape, Scoop stretched out both arms. He slipped one around the young woman's waist, the other, gingerly, around Summer. "Hold on to your rug, granpappy."

The mechanical man rose right up off the floor, leveled off at an altitude of twenty-five feet and flew them swiftly away from the scene of the altercation—just in time to miss the arrival of the green-clad security officers.

Leaning across Scoop's wide, highly polished chest, Vicky said, "Gee, Mr. Summer, I hope you don't mind this. What I mean is, you don't think I'm showing off, do you?"

"Not at all," he assured her.

4

The incredibly beautiful auburn-haired android smiled a dazzling smile and pulled up her Lycra tunic. "If you'll just look here, Mr. Summer," she requested.

Summer was just stowing his luggage in the wall bin of his compartment on the Westwood Deck of the immense *Hollywood II* spacecraft. One of the things he'd unpacked just before doing that was his palm-sized bugsniffer. "Be right with you." He grinned in the direction of the stunning andy's entirely believable breasts.

Built into her smooth, evenly tanned midsection was a rectangular vidscreen. "Let me ask you for your frank and candid opinion," requested the gorgeous mechanism. "You're a man known for his integrity and perception—or at least you used to be. We're wondering if this method of indoctrinating new passengers aboard the *Hollywood II* strikes you as being gauche."

Crouching, Summer swept the detecting gadget over the trim of his floating hydrobed. "Gauche isn't exactly the word I'd use."

"Tell me which word you would use."

"Cheesy."

His compact bugsniffer made a small pinging noise. There was an eardisc stuck to the underside of the neowood bed frame.

"That's ours," explained the android, blushing slightly. "As I told you, Mr. Summer, I'm with Public Relations. We don't always see eye to eye with Internal Security."

Nodding, he ground the listening device under his boot heel. "You have a vidtape to show me?"

"Yes, it's entitled *So You're Going to Travel Through the Limitless Infinity Of Space Aboard the Fabled* Hollywood II*!*"

"Catchy."

"You're being sardonic."

"Yep," he admitted as he continued checking out his compartment.

"Installing the viewscreen here"—she gestured gracefully to just below her breasts—"was PR's idea," she said. "There was some debate about which location would be the most effective. You'd be surprised what a variety of portions of the female anatomy are considered provocative. Trying to arouse the interest of the variety of guests we get from sundry planets and—"

The bugsniffer *binged*.

"Another one." Summer removed a wafer-thin minicam the size of a trubux coin from behind his wall mirror.

"Really? That isn't one of ours."

He held it between thumb and forefinger. "Looks like the brand the Barnum Drug Bureau uses." Dropping it, he stomped on it with his heel.

"Oh, them." She shook her blond head forlornly. "I thought those awful rumors had been laid to rest."

"Rumors about what?"

"You know, drug smuggling and all. Honestly, the public notion that anyone remotely connected with show business is a dope fiend or—"

"Maybe you better show me your movie."

"I get so mad when the media makes wild . . . Well, that's not why I'm here." She pressed her left nipple. The implanted screen blossomed to life. "If this really embarrasses you, I could send one of my colleagues. She's got the screen in her backside, since research indicates that 27% of humanoid males prefer—"

"This'll be fine." He eased the bathroom door open and began searching the off-white room for spy gadgets.

". . . *Hollywood II* is virtually a city in itself," a deep-voiced narrator was saying through the speaker in the lovely android's navel. "It houses thousands of well-adjusted people who are dedicated to traveling the length and breadth of this old universe of ours and making the best vidmovies for you and your family that's humanly, and otherwisely, possible to . . ."

"*Bing*," said the bugsniffer when Summer passed it over the sunken whirlbath unit.

He knelt, squinting. The latest bug was more complex than the others. "Huh . . . made out in the Hellquad planets looks like. Don't see that many hereabouts." He tossed it in the air a few times before dumping it down the floor dispozhole.

". . . a dozen vast sound stages with state-of-the-art movie-making equipment. And here we see the palatial Executive Level with its stately offices, acre upon acre of rolling sudograss, leafy . . ."

"Are you getting all this?" called the attractive andy.

"As much as I want, yes." He finished up the bath, moved on to the kitchen cubicle.

". . . the Writers' Hold, which is usually off limits to our average passenger . . ."

Summer found two real cockroaches in his zapstove, but no more spying gadgets in the kitchen or in the rest of his cabin.

". . . six regulation tennis courts, a freefall wrestling arena . . ."

Placing his bugsniffer on the edge of the floating glaz coffee table, Summer seated himself in a plaz slingchair. "An old associate of mine named Palma would enjoy your presentation," he told the android.

"Palma? Oh, yes, the horny photographer."

"Heard of him?"

"We have very extensive records on just about every media person in the universe."

". . . a most cordial and heartfelt welcome aboard!"

concluded the handsome-voiced narrator.

The auburn android's stomach went blank. "Thank you for your attention, Mr. Summer." She pulled down her tunic.

"Usually PR people call me Jack," he said. "I'm wondering why you—"

"Oh, that's in deference to your age. Anyone over thirty-five gets a Mister." Smiling prettily, she backed toward the doorway. "That applies to humanoids such as yourself. With other groups, of course, the cutoff age varies. Lizardmen, for example, live to be much—"

"Thanks for the indoctrination."

"Don't forget you're scheduled to sit in on a *Galaxy Jane* story conference at 3:15 PM/Ship Time," she reminded. "And I'll see you at the welcoming cocktail party. That's up on the Beverly Hills Deck at 5 PM/ST."

"Looking forward to both events."

"Well, I have three more passengers to welcome before we take off." She smiled again and let herself out. "Nice meeting you, Mr. Summer."

"Thirty-nine isn't especially old," he said aloud after she'd gone.

5

"Come in." Vicky yanked the door of her stateroom on the Bel Air Deck angrily open wide. "Boy, I'm really in a tizzy."

Summer entered the cabin, which was twice the size of his and smelled of wild flowers. "Don't say anything until—"

"Oh, if you mean the darn bug that somebody planted in here, we already found that thing." The blond young woman reached around him to give the neowood door a shove that caused it to shut with a shivering slam. "I complained to that dim-witted young android from PR who came around to show me a dippy movie about the *Hollywood II*. Gosh, he had the vidscreen built into the oddest—"

"One bug?"

"Relax, old timer." Scoop was sitting sideways in a tufted styrochair, metal legs dangling over the arm. "I checked the whole joint out. Got a detector built into my pinky."

"Even so." Taking his own bugsniffer from his pocket, Summer began a circuit of the parlor.

Vicky was wearing a two-piece white jeansuit and matching boots. "The thing that really annoys me is that this constitutes interference with the freedom of the press." She folded her arms under her breasts. "And that's something that's guaranteed in the constitutions of all the planets in the Barnum System except maybe—"

"*Bing*," said the gadget in Summer's hand.

Nodding, he reached up behind the tri-op painting of a field of grazing grouts. "Here's another," he said, flicking the spy device to the young woman.

Vicky caught it, brought it up close to her lips and shouted, "I hope this blows your darn eardrums out, you spying so and—"

"Relax, angelcake," said the camera robot. "I bet gramps here palmed that to impress you. I never miss a—"

"The Barnum Drug Bureau planted it," corrected Summer. "Apparently they stick 'em hither and yon aboard this spacecraft."

"They do? Then that means our tip about—"

"Stay mum," advised Summer as he headed for the next room.

"You don't expect to find more listening dornicks?" Vicky asked, following him. "What I mean is, Scoop is customized. Did I mention that already? The surveillance detecting gear he has built in to him sells at wholesale—wholesale, mind you—for a six-figure—"

"Let's get rid of that BDB one first." Retrieving it, he deposited the thing in the gold-rimmed dispozhole.

"Very impressive, the way you can still bend over like that, Summer," observed Scoop from his perch in the parlor. "Could be your body isn't yet as infirm as your brain."

"Want me to show you how to switch him off when he's not in use?" Summer offered, while circling the large oval bathpool on hands and knees.

"Oh, that's only his idea of good-natured kidding," said Vicky, watching Summer. "They built that into him. Journalistic badinage is the term for it."

"That's your term for . . . Ah, yeah." With the aid of the bugsniffer he located a third spying device. One that was very similar to the unidentifiable one he'd found in his own cabin. When Summer stood, his left knee made a faint crackling sound.

"I make no comment on that telltale noise," said Scoop. "I refrain from pointing out that old coots are noted for their creaking joints and bones. Which is only to be expected when you build with a calcium-based material rather than a dependable alloy like—"

"That's enough teasing," suggested Vicky.

After studying the device for a moment, Summer consigned it to the ship's disposal system. "Found one in my quarters, too."

"How the heck many people are interested in our digging into this Zombium smugg—"

"Wait."

She pressed her fingers to her lips. "More?"

Summer continued his search. Finally, after five more minutes of poking around, he said, "That seems to be all."

Vicky went back into the parlor to sit on the edge of the lucite sofa. "Okay, the first bug is probably courtesy of the *Hollywood II* security people. Right?"

"Yep."

"And you say the second one is from the Barnum Drug Bureau."

"More than likely, yes." He sat on a sudocanvas bucketchair. "It's that third bug I'm puzzled by."

She frowned. "You mean we might have somebody spying just on us?"

"I'll check out a few more cabins at random," Summer told her. "If it turns out you and I are the only ones with that extra spy device, then—"

"But nobody can know what we're really up to," she said. "What I mean is, at least a dozen other reporters and such boarded when the *Hollywood II* docked on Barnum. All to do writeups and vidreports on the making of *Galaxy Jane*. We're merely, far as anyone is supposed to know, more of the same. Why single us out for special—"

"That's one of the things," said Summer, "I'll have to find out."

Resting her palms on her knees, Vicky said, "I've been doing quite a lot of research on Zombium, Mr. Summer, and—"

"Start calling me Jack."

"Well, okay. It's just that I'm still sort of in awe of you," she said. "What I mean is, when I was still a kid in private school way off in the Earth System I was reading your wonderful pieces in *Muckrake*, which I had to sneak into my dorm because we—"

"Angelcake, this sort of gush'll rust my screws," complained Scoop, swinging his big metal feet to the parlor floor.

"We'll need some background footage," Summer said in the cambot's direction. "Now that the ship's taken off, you can roam the decks gathering—"

"Wait a sec, palsy walsy. I call my own shots on what gets filmed and—"

"Not this trip. So go on out and start—"

"Vicky, are you going to let this duffer order me—"

"Mr. Summer . . . Jack's in charge," said Vicky. "Run along and do some of that incisive filming you're noted for."

"I hate to leave you alone with this bozo." Slowly, with evident reluctance, Scoop rose from his chair. "Remember the info I got on him out of the NewzNet personnel files? He turns out to be near as bad as the crazed shutterbug he used to work with, especially when it comes to making passes at young, innocent maidens or even—"

"That'll be enough." She pointed at the door. "Stay away awhile, too."

"Okay, okay, I'll breeze." The robot opened the door. "Holler if he gets grabby." He left them.

"I apologize for Scoop," said the young woman. "Could be they put too much good-natured kidding in him. Anyway, we're both professionals, Jack, and I certainly feel more than safe alone with you."

"Most everybody does."

"I wasn't too familiar with Zombium until I got this assignment," she resumed. "In my schools alcohol and brainstimmers were much more popular than drugs like Zombium. It soulds like pretty dangerous stuff, though, from what I've been learning."

"Zombium is tricky," he said. "The first few times you use the stuff—orally in powdered form, usually—you just feel incredibly euphoric and untroubled."

"You ever tried any?"

He shook his head. "Nope, but I did a lot of research, talked to users, a few years back."

"Oh, that's right. I read that series in *Muckrake*," she said. "In fact, it was to you that Flo Haypenny admitted her longtime addiction to Zombium."

"And her cure."

"You think she'll be uneasy having you around while she's starring in *Galaxy Jane*?"

"Been years since all that happened."

Vicky said, "As I understand it, after the first few doses things can get worse."

"Usually, in order to keep the euphoria coming, you have to keep increasing the amount you take," he explained. "The stronger the dose the greater the chance of slipping into a deathlike trance. Again, the severity of the trances increase, too. Initial trances last from a few hours up to a day, but later on they can stretch to weeks or even months. And about a third of the longtime users rise up and walk around, somnambulist style, during the trances. Causing them no end of problems and accidents."

"According to the statistics in *The Galactic Guide to Licit & Illicit Drugs*, something like fourteen percent of long-term Zombium users never come out of their trances at all. They just stay that way until they die."

"Closer to twenty-five percent."

She shivered once. "That's sort of awful."

Summer stood. "It is," he agreed. "But smuggling and peddling the drug is also a great way to get rich. That makes the dealers, some of whom may well be sharing our trip on the fabled *Hollywood II* with us, nasty and rough. Especially when reporters come along who intend to futz up their business by doing video exposes."

"I understand that, yes, and I can look out for myself," she said, rising. "Although I am a little unsettled by Scoop's not finding those other bugs."

"Let's get to the story conference." He crossed to the doorway. "So we can start impressing all and sundry with how interested we are in the making of *Galaxy Jane*."

6

When the orange-feathered screenwriter leaped from his chair and up atop the conference table, trotted down half its length and attempted to throttle the handsome humanoid producer, the white-enameled public relations robot seated between Summer and Vicky down at their end of the long oval chuckled appreciatively. "This is what I mean about this picture being a lot of fun," he said.

"Women's angle!" cried the angry parrotman as he struggled to get a good feathery grip on the *Galaxy Jane* producer's smooth tanned throat. "Geeze, Gonzer, this is a goddamn pirate flicker!"

The PR 'bot put his white fingers to his metallic lips.

"They clown around like this all the live-long day."

"I noticed the scuff marks on the table," said Summer.

The husky cyborg headwriter, seated next to the struggling producer, inclined his aluminum right hand in the direction of his agitated parrot colleague. "I don't want to have to stun you again, Harl," he said. "Calm down and return to your chair, old buddy."

"Calm down! Calm down!" He left off his choking attempts. "We're scripting an epic here, Gunner! It's a sweeping saga of piracy and a gutsy plea for political understanding as regards the basic rights of the hungry and downtrodden—"

"Actually, gentlemen," remarked an obese toadman at midtable, "you've exaggerated the political situation in your script. True, Galaxy Jane did become modestly involved in an uprising among the Green Men of Gravespawn while residing for—"

"Modestly involved! Modestly involved!" Shedding feathers, the parrot man went clomping along the table top to where the immense toad was sitting. "We're talking, beanbrain, about a spiritual and moral revolution that profoundly affected a significant—"

"The motives of the renegade robot who led that longago revolt, this so-called Tin Mahatma, were nowhere so clearly defined as they appear in your rather simpleminded script, Mr. Grzyb. What you've failed—"

"Actually, Professor Bleistift," said the cyborg author across the table, "I wrote most of the scenes dealing with the native uprising against the imperialistic—"

"Um," said the pudgy blond young man who was sitting on the far side of Vicky. "All you folks keep throwing around terms like imperialistic, which tends to make it look as though my great grandfather—the illustrious Captain Thatcher King of the Royal Mounted Stungunners—was some sort of unsavory tool of an oppressive government. It's bad enough, really, that your shabby script paints him as a twit who was shacking up with some unkempt lady crook. But when you further—"

"There's considerable evidence," put forth the toad professor, "that the captain did indeed carry on an affair with Galaxy Jane. As historical consultant on this important vidmovie I'd be neglecting my office did I not correct your—"

"A lot you know," said the pudgy young man, rising off his glaz chair. "My mom sent you highly legible faxcopies of my great granddad's journals. And there's not one entry from the period we're talking about in which he says a thing about fooling around with your Galaxy Jane or any other lady space pirate. Fact is, he habitually refers to her as 'The Scourge of the Spaceways.' That, I hardly have to point out, isn't a term of endearment or—"

"Captain King's wife back home," said the handsome producer as he massaged his neck. "I like her. I see her sitting by the fireplace. Right, sitting by the fireplace with this journal open on her lap. And she's trying to read between the lines. Is her husband nurfing this pirate bimbo? Tears touch her—"

"My great-grandfather was entirely faithful. He rarely even—"

"The half-witted wife isn't even in our script," yelled Harlan Grzyb, hopping up and down in the middle of the big oval table. "This is another dumb example of how you're turning this meaningful—"

Zzzzzzummmmmmm!

The headwriter used the stungun built into his thumb.

Grzyb stiffened, shed a small swirl of bright orange feathers, took two wobbly steps to his left and then fell over onto the toad professor.

The PR robot masked another amused chuckle with his white fingers. "These guys really give me a kick," he said. "Kidding around from dawn to dusk. I hope you people take this joshing in the spirit in which it's int—"

"Thanks, Gunner," said the producer.

"He's young and he gets excited." Gunner Hock left

his chair, grabbed his unconscious colleague by the collar of his neotweed sportunic and lifted him clear of Professor Bleistift. "You can't convince the kid this is just a job." He carried Grzyb over into a corner and dropped him on the thermocarpet. "Myself, Shifty, I'm commencing to love your troubled wife at home angle."

"Sure, it's another good women's angle," said Shifty Gonzer, smiling. "That never hurts our box office."

"We put that together with the crippled daughter and we'll—"

"Wait now," said the blond young man. "There weren't any handicapped people in the King family. My great-grandfather's only daughter was, in point of fact, a famous tapdancer on the planet Barafunda in her day. She was graceful as a—"

"She's only lame actually," said the handsome Gonzer. "Then when Captain King recites this little prayer given to him by the Tin Mahatma we cut to her at home and she throws away her—"

"Sir," said Professor Bleistift, clearing his throat, "a certain amount of license is certainly tolerable. However, I must remind you that Captain King and the Tin Mahatma were sworn enemies. Also, please recall, the religion the Tin Mahatma preached was not a gentle or forgiving one. A typical prayer among his followers ran . . . hum . . . 'Oh, Evil and Bloody Goddess of Death and Terror, send Swift and Painful Death to All who oppose our Sacred Cause! Aiiieeee! Kill! Kill!' Hardly the thing to cure a lame tapdancer."

"Granny Alice wasn't crippled, she wasn't even lame," protested the King great-grandson.

"You people don't, yet, understand the women's angle," Hock told them, scratching his copper nose with an aluminum finger.

Gonzer was scowling in his chair at the table's head. "If we stun his schmuck during a story conference, does that futz up any of our agreements with the King family?"

Hock glanced around the big table. "We could put Bunker King, Jr. to sleep, Shifty. Legally, that is," he said. "With these press people here sitting in, though, we better go easy. Don't you think so, Jack?"

Summer said, "Right, Gunner. We wouldn't be favorably impressed."

"It's bad enough you put poor Mr. Grzyb into a stupor," said Vicky, angry. "I happen to have read several of the novels he wrote before he sold out to your people and he's a brilliant writer. His *I Have No Perch, Yet I Must Sing* is the best bird novel written on our—"

"Bird novels?" Gonzer bounced once in his chair and gazed at her. "We're trying to save a 90,000,000 trubux production and this skwack is giving me bird fiction."

"Nugent," said Hock, leaning in the producer's direction.

"Hum?"

"She's Victoria Nugent. Youngest daughter of Eli 'NewzNet' Nugent."

After three seconds Gonzer turned his scowl to a smile. "Excuse my illiterate remarks, Miss Nugent."

"If you ask me," said Vicky, avoiding Summer's mild nudge in the direction of her ribs, "poor unconscious Mr. Grzyb's great novel *Dangerous Birdcages* would make a heck of better vidmovie than this dippy yarn about Galaxy—"

"I don't agree there, miss," said Bunker King, Jr. "My great-grandfather's life is one of inspiring and admirable incident, his story should inspire young and old alike all across this universe of ours."

"Plus it's got a great women's angle," added Summer.

7

It was always twilight down on the Sunset Strip Deck and you got the feeling that the multitude of neon lights had just turned on and the best part of the evening was ahead of you. Or at least you were supposed to feel that.

Summer, alone again, was pretty much ignoring the flashing signs—*Kit Kat Klub, Swan Club, Avuncular Avram's Deli, Teensex Pavillion, Fred's Pharmacy, Garden of Allah*—and the glittering denizens. He went striding rapidly along, making his way through the strolling mix of actors, actresses and studio workers.

When he came to the Club Troc, he left the sidewalk and stepped into the deeper dimness inside. Except for three lizardmen extras in cowboy costumes, the small nightclub was empty of patrons. Behind the ebony bar crouched a chubby catman. He wore a one-piece checkered cazsuit and had a white apron wrapped around his middle. His fur was the color of peanut butter and had been slicked down with a hair tonic that smelled strongly of jungle wild flowers. Three jeweled rings showed on each furry paw, an emerald hoop dangled from his left ear.

Summer sat on a bar stool. "Evening, Onetime."

The slick-furred bartender glanced up at him. "They don't call me that anymore, Jack," he said in his gargly voice. "My current handle is Twice Obelisky."

"Congratulations."

Obelisky gave a purring smile. "Happened only five months ago," he explained, running the bar rag absently along the part in his head fur. "She was a real looker, too, except for . . . But I better not confide my escapade in you or it'll end up in the pages of *Muckrake*."

"Don't work for them anymore."

"No kidding?"

"With NewzNet."

"Still digging up dirt, though."

"Not this time," Summer said. "Just doing a vid feature on the making of *Galaxy Jane*."

"A turkey I hear. Hasn't got a strong enough women's angle." He reached beneath the bar, yanked up a siphon. "Still drinking sparkling water?"

"Yep."

"On the house." He fizzed the drink into a plaz glass.

"Thanks," said Summer. "When you worked in Bimbo's 440 down on Barnum, Twice, you were a knowledgeable fellow."

"For a fee, sure."

"Obviously."

"It's a thousand trubux now."

"What am I paying the extra five hundred for, the ambiance?"

"The state of the interplanetary economy has changed, Jack." He toyed with his earring. "What are you interested in?"

"Where can I get Zombium?"

Obelisky asked, "How's that tie in with the *Galaxy Jane* flicker?"

"If you ask me questions, I'll charge you a fee."

"Settle for mummydust," advised the catman. "Gives the same high as Zombium and, being a synthetic, you have no risk of—"

"Aboard this ship," persisted Summer, "where can I buy Zombium?"

"Got me." He gave a negative shake of his head, which caused a splat of hair oil to fly from his crown to the slick bar top near Summer's hand. "Like I say, mummydust's no problem. You can get plenty right on this level of the ship. And, with a little extra effort, moonshine, brainstim, headboxes, needlework, or even a sleeve job. But as for Zombium, that's rough. I got no idea, Jack."

Summer slid his glass over on top of the spot of pungent hair tonic. "Find out, Twice," he suggested. "Be worth two thousand."

"How long you aboard for?"

"Week at least."

"I'll inquire."

"Splendid."

"Should my luck hold," said Obelisky, "by this time next year you may be calling me Three Times."

Vicky took hold of Summer's arm, smiled and kissed him on the cheek. "I'm just pretending," she whispered, "in case we're under surveillance at this darn cocktail party."

"We undoubtedly are."

They were standing near the shallow end of the large oval swimming pool. Behind them the glaz wall of the large crowded room gave a believable view of wooded hills and stately homes.

"Name your poison, folks," requested the Thinkadrink robot that came rolling up to them. "Name your poison."

Summer said, "Sparkling water."

"That happens to be, you won't mind my saying, a sissy drink," said the servo, drumming copper fingers on the single nozzle protruding from his tanklike chest. "Those two gossips from *Interplanetary Movieland*—see them? Pudgy gatorman in the glocaftan and the bird bimbo with the beak ring?—just ordered a Venusian Boilermaker and a Calgary Eye-opener. Now, that's my idea of drinks that'll—"

"I'd like," said Vicky, "a nearbeer."

"You're spoofing me? The only nearbeer I've poured thus far was for that Galactic Girl Scout who's covering *Galaxy Jane* for her orbiting middle school newsp—"

"Do you float?" inquired Summer.

"Is that a drink you're asking for? Like a root beer—"

"Nope, I was curious as to what'd happen when you fell in yonder pool." Summer grinned. "My guess is you'd sink."

"I bet he'd float," said Vicky. "For a while anyway."

"Sure, sure, I get it." The Thinkadrink opened his side, extracted two licorice-tinted plaz glasses. "Surly drunks I'm more than accustomed to, but surly teetotalers . . . One nearbeer . . . uck . . . and one sparkling water for you, Percy."

"Much obliged," said Summer, taking the drink.

As soon as the servo had rolled off to accost a table of stuntmen, Vicky said quietly, "That happens to be Ezra Zilber over near the Plutonian Smorgasbord on the other side of the pool, the sort of moderately swishy catman in the two-piece candy-stripe funsuit."

"Yep, I spotted him just before you arrived."

"But he hasn't contacted you yet?"

"Not so far," replied Summer. "Shortly I'll talk to him."

"I'd have thought, since he's the one who contacted NewzNet in the first place, that he'd have been in touch with you before this."

"According to Taliaferro, Zilber is reluctant to have anything more to do with us. He'd prefer to have us find out about the Zombium smuggling and then just collect the rest of his tip fee when the story breaks."

"Well, we may not even need Zilber." Vicky took a sip of her nearbeer. "Hey, this tastes like soda pop. Did I get your drink by mistake?"

"Everything the Thinkadrink 'bots pour tastes like soda pop," he told her. "Basic flaw in the machines. What do you mean we won't need him?"

"I've been doing some undercover work on my own.

You know, dropping into sleazy bars down on the Strip Deck, hinting that I'm a dippy heiress who wants to make a Zombium buy. So far—"

"You are a dippy heiress, if you think you can mess directly with—"

"I'm certainly not intruding on your investigating, Jack. All I'm doing is supplementing your—"

"Damn it, Vicky, this has nothing to do with professional ethics," he said. "What I'm worried about is your getting killed."

"I appreciate your concern for my well-being, but—"

"Forget your well-being. If somebody knocks you off it could futz up this whole deal."

"Oh." She took a slow, deep breath. "Well, I'm sorry I—"

"Let me decoy the dealers," he said. "And let me contact Zilber."

"Okay." Turning, she walked forlornly away from him.

"That's surprising."

Summer turned to see Flo Haypenny, an attractive red-haired woman of thirty some years, sitting alone at a floating table a few yards away. "You're unchanged, Flo," he said, crossing to the small circular table.

"Now that's exactly what I mean." Flo smiled up at him. "That's the Jack Summer I remember. Charming, always there with the blarney. Not the kind of man who sends pretty young girls off in tears."

He took the seat opposite her, setting his glass on a coaster that featured a tri-op photo of her decked out as Galaxy Jane and brandishing a pair of kilguns. "That was Vicky Nugent."

"Daughter of Eli?"

"This is her first assignment out of school," he explained, glancing at the tall glass of green liquid near her hand. "She's nervous, that's all."

"Maybe that explains why she walked off on you. I didn't think many . . . it's peppermint soda, Jack. I'm still okay and staying away from anything dangerous."

"That I can see."

"You were very helpful back then," said the red-haired actress. "It was a rough time for all concerned."

Summer nodded, said nothing.

Flo asked, "Can I help you with what you're working on now?"

"You can, sure. I'd like to talk to you about *Galaxy Jane,* about how you see the character and—"

"I meant what you're really working on."

Grinning, he shook his head. "I'm mellowing as I grow older, Flo. Really. All I'm interested in is a simple six-to-eight-minute segment on how an epic gets made."

She poked her tongue into her cheek, watching him for a few silent seconds. "I'd like to talk to you about something anyway," she said finally. "There are a few things going on aboard the *Hollywood II* that you ought to know about."

"You're on the Bel Air Deck?"

"Villa 26. About 11 tonight?"

"That'll be—"

"You better go look after your pretty partner," suggested the actress. "The Swain Brothers are attempting to charm her."

"Who're they?" He stood, spotted Vicky talking to a pair of bright green young men in three-piece silvery cazsuits.

"Very gifted fellows, in charge of our Special Effects Department. They also own a piece of the whole ship and all the productions," she said. "They're also nearly as horny as that old photographer partner of yours, though nowhere near as amiable."

"I'll try a few of my own special effects on them if need be." He made his way toward the other side of the pool.

Vicky was backed against a potted palm and the two chuckling green men were, so it looked from this distance, tickling her.

Summer nodded at Gunner Hock as he circled the group the cyborg screenwriter was dominating. He avoided another eager Thinkadrink, stepping around a lovely catgirl who was dangling her bare feet in the pool.

"You are Summer? No? Yes?"

"Yes, as a matter of fact." A huge lizardman had lunged in front of him. "Right now, though, I have—"

"My name—perhaps you know it already? Yes? No?—my name is Dr. Harvey J. Gummox. I happen to be the ship's physician." There was a foamy flagon of Murdstone green ale in his hand.

"Pleased to meet you, Dr. Gummox. Later on I'd like to chat with you about—"

"Tonight. In my suite on the Malibu Deck," said the big lizard physician. "Shall we say midnight. Yes? No?"

"Let's first say—why?"

"I talk, you listen," said Gummox. "I believe I have some information that a noted muckraking reporter such as yourself—"

"This particular jaunt isn't a muckraking one, doctor," said Summer. "Still, it won't hurt to have a chat. Midnight." He moved free and continued on his way toward the beleaguered Vicky.

"But we can't help ourselves," insisted one of the bright green Swains as he attempted to slide an arm around her slim waist.

"You inspire us," claimed the other, reaching for her elbow.

Vicky bobbed and weaved. "Guys, quit."

"The very gents I'm seeking," said Summer amiably when he reached them. "We want to interview you two gifted lads about your special effects for *Galaxy Jane*. As I understand it your Tin Mahatma is a life-sized triumph of—"

"Who's this gink, Slim?"

"Search me, Slam."

"He's Jack Summer," introduced Vicky as she

caught hold of Summer's arm. "We're colleagues."

Slam Swain eyed him. "I've heard a good deal about you, Summer," he admitted.

"So have I," muttered Slim Swain. "You're supposed to be one rough and nasty bozo."

"All I'm interested in now, fellows, is an inter—"

"We'll maybe," said Slim, backing away, "have time for something like that after we land on Murdstone."

"See us then," added Slam. "Be sure to bring your fetching cohort along."

Obviously disheartened, the two emerald siblings drifted elsewhere.

"Thanks for intervening," said the blond young woman.

"That's what colleagues are for." Sensing something behind him, he turned.

Standing next to a potted palm, and partially concealed by it, was Ezra Zilber. "This is all dreadfully awkward." He brushed at his cheek whiskers with a nervous paw.

"We have to talk," said Summer. He strolled, casually over to the palm.

"Not here, not here. It's much too horribly public. I shouldn't even be approaching you now, but you've been eying me all through the—"

"Suggest a place."

"Meet me on Sound Stage 6, the *Haunted Mansion* set," said the uneasy catman. "That's one of the productions I'm doing set designs for, so if we're seen there it won't look too awfully suspicious."

"What time?"

"Oh, 10 PM tonight," said Zilber. "You might tell your Mr. Taliaferro, when next you communicate, that I am frightfully miffed at having to have direct contact with you people."

"There'll be a bonus."

"A terribly small one if I know NewzNet." The palm fronds quivered as he went, hurriedly, away.

Summer returned to Vicky's side. "Looks like I've got a rich full evening ahead of me," he said.

8

The four-armed green cyclops winked, adjusted his soiled chefhat, scratched at one of his left armpits, pointing across the small cafe. "Is it possible for youse to see the grill from your booth here?"

"Not at all, nope," answered Summer.

"But we can smell it," said Vicky, who was sitting across the linotopped table.

"That's real pork lard." The green proprietor of Bugeye's Beanery fished an order pad from the lumpy pocket in his soiled apron. "Youse are whiffing real pork lard sizzling on that grill. That guarantees that youse are going to enjoy *authentic* Earth-style cuisine. Lots of other joints here on the Santa Monica Deck claim to feature Earth-style cookery. Only Bugeye's Beanery, however, gives youse the real thing."

"I'll just have," said Summer, "a cup of nearcaf."

Bugeye's brow lowered. "Aren't youse up to experiencing the joys of authentic—"

"Fix me a burger, well done," said Vicky. "I'd like a side order of fries—make that a double order—a dish of coleslaw, a chocolate malted, a wedge of apple pie and a cola with plenty of crushed ice."

The green man chuckled appreciatively. "Now youse are obviously a lady who appreciates the absolute best of the culinary arts of the faroff planet Earth. Wish I could say the same for your date."

"He has a nervous stomach," she explained.

"Would youse, miss, care to come back behind the counter to watch me fry the fries in authentic grease—teleported daily from the Earth System?"

"Maybe next time."

Bugeye straightened his soiled white hat, hitched up his soiled white apron, scratched another armpit and picked a canine tooth with the tip of his electropen. "I'll return to my grill."

Vicky rested both elbows on the table top. "You really will end up with a nervous stomach, Jack, if you overwork yourself the way you're planning—"

"Talking with three people over the course of a couple hours isn't—"

"I can see, sort of, where you'd want to visit Flo Haypenny alone," she said. "What I mean is, you probably had a torrid romance with her back when and—"

"I don't have torrid romances with anybody, especially ladies I'm doing stories about."

"You forget I was briefed on your past before I—"

"Nevertheless."

"What I'm getting at, Jack, is there's no reason I can't help you question Zilber or this Dr. Gumpox. After all—"

"Gummox."

"Afterall, I'm very good at interviewing. I mean—and I know you think it's kid stuff and in a way it is, but even so—I won the prestigious Platt Award for Incisive Interviewing two semesters in a—"

"Zilber is scared," Summer reminded her. "He doesn't really want to talk to anyone. So I'm not going to come at him with a team of—"

"Only you and me. It's not as though we're dragging along Scoop and—"

"Where is your charming customized cambot, by the way? He was only at the cocktail party for about fifteen minutes."

"Wait'll you see the footage. Scoop can just come in, size up a situation and then—"

"Where is he at this very moment?"

Vicky rubbed a splotch of something greenish off her plaz-covered menu. "I really wish you shared my opinion of his—"

"Where?"

"The Sunset Strip Deck. I figure we're going to need some footage of that once we expose the—"

"Marvelous." Summer slouched some. "Subtle, too. 'Hi, I'm the NewzNet roving robot. Are you a Zombium smuggler?' "

"He's very deft and careful."

"Yeah, I noticed."

Vicky inhaled slowly, exhaled rapidly. "You're avoiding the real issue here," she accused. "I think I can at least share the Dr. Gummox interview with—"

"This isn't an interview. The guy probably wants to sell me some information."

"That's not very ethical of him, since he's a doctor."

Nodding, Summer said, "That's why he'll want as few witnesses as possible."

"Yes, but—"

"There youse go, miss. Burger and all the trimmings." Bugeye set the plate before her, plumped the cola glass next to it, set Summer's cup of steaming nearcaf in front of him and passed Vicky the plazcruet of ketchup sub. "Take a gander, if youse will, at those sliced gherkins. Spaced in daily from the planet Esmeralda."

"The gherkin capital of the universe," said Summer.

Leaning closer to the young woman, Bugeye inquired,

"Youse and this guy romantically linked?"

"Just good friends."

"That's a relief," he sighed. "My advice, miss, would be never to get too entangled with a wiseass."

"Sound advice." She picked up a plump greasy fry.

"Words to live by." Bugeye withdrew.

Vicky ate three fries. "The grease does make a difference," she observed. "By the way, Jack, why did your wife leave you?"

"She was an inch taller than me." He sipped his nearcaf.

"No, what was really involved?"

"I was an inch shorter than she."

"You don't much want to talk about her?"

"I'm starting to see why you won that Platt loving cup. You perceive right off what—"

"Not a cup. It's a sort of a lopsided block of . . . um . . . lucite, I think." Picking up her burger, she took a careful bite. "Was she pretty?"

"Ravishing."

"And you loved her?"

"Desperately."

"Then why did you break up?"

"It was mostly because—and I've never confided this in anyone, Vicky, until tonight—it was a culinary thing," he answered. "She developed a fondness for Earth-style burgers and fries. After a while, though I fought against it, the continual scent of pork fat around our love nest got—"

"All right, okay. I'll save the rest of my queries for a later time," said Vicky, taking another bite of the burger. "But he's sure darn right about you."

"Who?"

"Bugeye," she said. "You really are a wiseass."

9

The old dark house stood on a hill, shielded by a grove of gnarled trees. The grass on the hillside was nearly knee-high and completely believable.

Summer, using a small lightrod to guide himself through the deserted sound stage, climbed carefully up the hill. He'd noticed a flicker of light at one of the windows of the ramshackle mansion and assumed the uneasy Ezra Zilber was waiting for him in there.

Each of the seven neowood steps creaked as Summer climbed to the rickety porch.

He halted on the wide porch, watching the half-open doorway a few feet away. There was no sign of light inside now.

He moved to a lame chair and turned it to face the rectangle of darkness. He sat down.

The mansion made a few faint creaking sounds.

Then the carved neowood door started to swing farther inward.

"This is horribly nerve-wracking," said Zilber, hidden in the darkness of the house.

"It is sort of stressful," said Summer. "You coming out or shall I come in?"

"Stay there," cautioned the nervous catman. "I'll remain here, where I don't feel so frightfully exposed."

"You told NewzNet this spaceship's being used to smuggle Zombium."

"It is, yes."

"Proof?"

"The last time we were doing location work on Murdstone, that was four months ago during the shooting of *Galactic Cowboys*," said the unseen Zilber, "I chanced to go into a seldom used prop storage warehouse down on the San Pedro Deck. I noticed two crates that hadn't been . . . What was that sound?''

''House settling probably.''

''I feel so terribly vulnerable, blurting this out in full view of—''

''Nobody, including me, can see you,'' Summer assured him. ''There was Zombium in those crates?''

''I only dared open one, but that is what was in it.''

''You're sure?''

''Certainly. In my youth I flirted with the awful stuff,'' the catman said. ''There was at least a hundred pounds of Zombium in that crate, Summer. That means a resale value of millions of trubux. I became so horribly upset that I didn't risk opening the other, and I shut the first one up tight and labored to make sure no one would guess it'd ever been tampered with.''

''Who put the crates there?''

''I'm not sure.''

''But you have a hunch.''

''Well, if it's all the same to you, I'd rather forget all this whole and entire business. I was horribly foolish to have approached NewzNet in the—''

''What happened to the two crates?''

''When I looked again two days later, they were gone.''

''Who took them?''

''I really don't know.''

Summer said, ''Be worth another 5000 trubux to have a name.''

''I really don't intend to meet a gruesome end for 5000.''

''Ten thousand then.''

After a few thoughtful seconds Zilber asked, ''Could you give me half of that up front?''

''Nope.'' He reached inside his jacket. ''But I can slip you 1000.''

''Two thousand.''

''One thousand.''

"Very well. But I must say you're being horribly chintzy."

"True." He eased out his groutskin wallet and extracted a 1000 trudollar bill.

"Could you pass it in to me?"

Leaving his chair, Summer held the money out toward the darkened doorway.

A furry hand darted out, grabbed the bill and took it back into the darkness.

Summer asked, "You suspect somebody specific?"

"There are, let's say, a few suspicions I can follow up on."

"I'll contact you again tomorrow."

"No, I'll contact you."

"Do it by this time tomorrow, or I'll come hunting for you."

"There's no need for that. Good night."

Summer stood on the porch for a few moments before leaving.

Dropping his bugsniffer back in his pocket, Summer said, "Now we can talk."

Flo Haypenny was sitting on a glaz sofa that was filled with pale blue water and hundreds of tiny swimming exotic fish. "Two spy devices in my villa. I'm flattered."

"I found three in my compartment," he said. "Only the news people seem to get that extra one."

The red-haired actress, who was wearing a two-piece green skirtsuit now, smiled. "I'm glad you dropped by," she said. "Since I missed you at the cocktail party, I—"

"Flo, I dropped the bugs down the dispozhole," he told her.

"I know, I saw you do that." A puzzled look touched her face. Behind her the wide-view window showed a convincing stretch of night forest.

"So you don't have to pretend you didn't invite me here."

Her eyes widened. "I don't think I understand, Jack. Are you joking about something I don't—"

"We did talk at the party." Leaving his tin slingchair, he crossed the thick thermocarpet to stand over her.

That frightened the fish inside the sofa. They began to swim around in an agitated flickering way—scarlet ones, emerald ones, seablue ones—turning the water foamy.

The actress pressed her fingers to her forehead. "No, I don't remember anything like that."

He sat down close beside her. "You told me there were disturbing things happening on the *Hollywood II*."

"I did?" She shook her head. "I really have no recollection of that."

"You were worried about something, Flo. What exactly has been going on to—"

"That's just it," she said. "Nothing's worrying me. This has been a relaxed trip so far. The rehearsals went smoothly. Frank Yoe is flubbing a mimimum of his lines during our shooting of the interior scenes."

"And you really don't remember talking to me?"

"No." She was frowning. "I'm not taking anything these days, Jack. At that damn cocktail gathering I drank nothing but a couple of soft drinks."

"I know."

She took his hand. "You were one of the few people I could count on . . . back when I was having all my troubles," she said. "Okay, I know I'm not drugged or drunk. Then why don't I remember?"

"There were a hundred people at the party," he said. "One of them must've overheard you inviting me to come by and talk."

"What are you getting at? That someone did something to me?" Her fingers tightened around his.

"A brainwipe probably."

"But who'd do that?"

"I don't know yet."

She closed her eyes. "I still remember my lines for tomorrow's shooting," she said, opening her eyes.

"Brainwipes can be selective," he said. "This one just took away what you wanted to tell me and the fact you'd had a conversation about being worried."

"You're still an investigative reporter, aren't you? When they told me you were aboard just to do a vidreport about *Galaxy Jane,* I had my doubts."

Summer said, "I'm interested in more than just your movie."

"But you're not going to tell me much about it."

"Be safer if I don't."

Flo said, "This someone—this someone who did this to me—he had to come in here to do that."

"Most likely."

"Someone was here, using a brainwipe gadget on me—telling me what I had to forget—and I don't have any recollection at all."

"Whoever it is doesn't want to harm you," he said. "Just prevent you from telling me about certain things."

"Damn, I wish I knew what . . . A few hours ago I did and now . . . Jack, I don't like feeling this way," she said. "It's really too much like it was back when I was taking so much Zombium and waking up with no—"

"Easy now." He put his arm around her shoulders.

"Could you stay here?"

"For a while."

"I meant all night."

"Can't. There are more people I have to talk to yet."

"This all sounds dangerous."

"Odds are it is, yes."

"They may not use a brainwipe on you, they may just try to kill you."

"Yes, my dear, it's a risky trade I've chosen. Fraught with perils and—"

"All right, okay," she said. "You don't want to be serious anymore."

"Been my experience that being serious doesn't much help in situations like this."

"Probably not." She kissed him.

"Snerg embryos," explained Dr. Gummox, with a sweeping gesture at the row of jars on his mantel. "A passion of mine."

"And mighty decorative." Summer settled into the inflated rubberoid armchair across from the huge lizard physician.

Gummox was decked out in a flowered neosilk lounging robe and had an unlit pipe in his mouth. "I am, by training, a surgeon," he said. "Although there's little call for that aboard the *Hollywood II*. I have, if you follow me, retained the surgeon's habit of cutting to the heart of the matter. You comprehend? Yes? No?"

"What you want to do is get right down to business."

"Exactly. Your network has an enormous amount of money to spend."

"Quite a lot." Summer glanced away from the mantel, taking in the glittering jumble of medical tools on the dark metal shelves across the parlor. "They tend, though, to spend it very conservatively."

The doctor shifted his considerable bulk and his inflated sofa made a protesting sigh. "You are more than just a showbiz reporter?"

"I work in other areas sometimes."

"Scandal. That is an area of interest to you?"

"Might be. Depending on who's involved."

Taking the dead pipe from his mouth, the lizard leaned forward. "Stars of the cinema."

"Stars who're on the *Hollywood II* right now?"

"As you suggest."

"If you supply information that leads to something, doctor, NewzNet'll pay you 1000 trubux."

Snorting, Gummox sat up straight. "You intend to insult me? Yes? No?"

"One thousand's our standard fee. But you might have something that's worth more."

"I do. A first-rate scandal."

Grinning, Summer asked, "Could you maybe hint at what it is?"

"It involves," the greenish doctor said, "illegal drugs."

"Something like Zombium?"

Dr. Gummox flinched. "Perhaps," he admitted. "Illegal drugs and very important people."

"You have proof?"

"I will tell you how to obtain proof."

"Two thousand, tops." Summer stood up.

"That is still an insult."

"I'll get back to you tomorrow." He walked to the parlor door.

"This particular scandal is worth, at a minimum, 10,000."

"Not to me," Summer told him.

10

Bunker King, Jr. yelled, "Cut!"

The toadman director leaped clear out of his plaz-chair. "What in blue blazes do you think you're doing?"

"Well sir, Mr. Chiizu," said the blond young man, making his way toward him through the tangle of wires and cables on the sound-stage floor, "this scene you're shooting here makes my great-grandfather look like a sissy."

"And what, may I ask," inquired Kedju Chiizu, scowling greenly, "is wrong with sissies?"

"Nothing, I suppose, except there's never been one in our family—if you overlook Uncle Mel and we were never absolutely certain about him."

The set replicated, in completely believable terms, the interior of a cave on the planet Murdstone. The cave was supposed to be on the edge of a desert. Wind and sand machines were howling away. Within the cave Captain Thatcher King of the Royal Mounted Stungunners, handsome in his blue and gold uniform, faced the Tin Mahatma. Captain King was being portrayed by Francis X. Yoe, a tanned actor of thirty-seven. The Mahatma, a silvery robot clad in a yellow robe, was a technical triumph of the Swain Brothers. The two green-skinned siblings were crouched at a complex control panel just out of camera range.

"I'm losing my mood," mentioned Yoe. "These crying scenes are hard to do, you know. Particularly difficult when the script calls for 'heartrending sobs.' That's a toughy. I thought about that a lot while preparing last night. How do I rend my heart when I sob? I gave a—"

"Not *your* heart, gooberbrain," cried Harlan Grzyb from the sidelines. "You don't want to rend your heart, but rather the hearts of the poor hapless boobs who're going to view this dim-witted travesty of the once brilliant script we—"

"He ought not," insisted young King, "to be sobbing at all."

"He's showing this crazed rebel leader the photos of his poor maimed daughter," reminded the toad director, impatiently. "Even an oxlike dolt such as your great-grandfather is going to blubber when—"

"She wasn't maimed."

"We have footage in Research showing the old girl hobbling around like—"

"Those particular pictures were taken at a family picnic, after she'd just finished participating in a three-legged race. Naturally she—"

"Do we want any of this?" whispered Vicky in Summer's ear.

"We probably have more than we need," he replied.

They were standing behind the row of three movie-camera robots, watching the interrupted scene.

"Guess I really am a born journalist," the young woman said. "Worrying about this fake vidreport as though it weren't merely a cover for the more serious—"

"Let's not discuss that out here in the open."

"Hey, this looks like fun." Scoop left them, hurrying closer to the set as Grzyb stretched up, shedding a few feathers, to punch the director on his green jaw.

"I doubt I'm going to be able to cry at all," said Yoe, "unless we start shooting this pretty—"

"Relax, sweetie," droned the Tin Mahatma, lurching and giving him an enthusiastic hug.

"Grandfather never embraced a robot," shouted King.

"Just kidding around," explained Slam Swain from

the Mahatma control panel. "Breaks the tension, we've found."

"Right," added Slim Swain, "a little levity clears the air."

Somebody touched Summer in the small of the back. He spun and found himself facing a birdman gaffer in a one-piece worksuit. "Something?"

"Thrice Obelisky sends a message."

"Thrice?"

"So he claims," said the yellow-feathered stagehand. "He suggests you be at Jukebox Charlie's on the Malibu Deck at 7 tonight."

"Okay, I will."

"Take care." The gaffer drifted away.

Hildy took hold of Summer's arm. "Was that what I think it was?"

"Don't know. What do you think it was?"

"One of your contacts aboard this spacecraft wants to pass some vital information on to—"

"Nothing vital probably."

"Whatever it is, I really think I ought to accompany you on this—"

"Nope."

"The darn Malibu Deck isn't very dangerous, Jack. Not like the Sunset—"

"The people we're interested in are dangerous. I'll go on this one alone."

"I wish I were a bit more like Harlan Grzyb."

"Oh, so?"

"Then I could," she explained, "punch you in the kisser when you make me angry."

Jukebox Charlie had a small, colorful jukebox built into his wide chest. He was a curly-haired human, heavy-set and about five years older than Summer. "It drives the ladies wild," he was pointing out from the table they shared near the tinted viewindow of his beachside cafe. "Admittedly the sound quality isn't all it could be, but they just love to drop coins in my slot."

"How often do you change the selections?" asked Summer.

"That's all handled by the jukebox company. I don't have much choice," Jukebox Charlie replied. "Right now I'm very heavy on Electronic Polkas from Jupiter, which isn't my idea of the sort of mood music you need for a bistro such as—"

"Thrice says you—"

"How about that guy changing his name again so quick? If you ask me he bought this latest piece of—"

"Are you the one I have to see to buy some—"

"Naw, I don't deal in drugs." He nodded at the stretch of twilight beach outside. "See that little boat house next to that rickety yet picturesque pier?"

A dim yellowish light showed at the windows of the ramshackle neowood building. "Yep."

"You meet the fella there."

Summer pushed back in his chair. "Been a pleasure meeting—"

"Want to play something? On the house. Just got some nice tenor ballads from Murdstone that'll bring a tear to—"

"I'm anxious to keep my appointment." Grinning, he left the table.

The surf was very believable. It came hissing in across the authentic sand as simulated twilight deepened all around him.

Summer cut across the beach, avoiding the reach of the foamy tide. A plump seagull perched on a nearby piling, eying him with a minimum of interest.

Halting, Summer took a glance back the way he'd come. Shadows were thickening on the twisting path down the brush-covered hillside. Eyes narrowed, he scanned the scrub and then, with a slight shrug, continued on his way.

He walked out along the short neowood pier, weathered planks creaking underfoot. A few yards from the rectangle of yellow light that marked the half-open doorway of the boat house he stopped and called, "Ahoy."

"Summer?" The voice was deep and raspy.

"The same."

"C'mon in," invited the voice, "and we'll work out something."

He resumed walking.

The door swung all the way inward just before he reached it.

He crossed the threshold onto the plank floor.

There didn't seem to be anybody inside the room.

Somebody dropped on him from above.

A furry arm locked around his neck, another gripped him across the chest. "We don't like muckrakers, Summer."

"So I gather." Twisting in the catman's powerful grasp, he kicked backward and up with one booted foot.

"Oof! We also don't like bastards who try to kick us in the goonies."

Summer kicked again, elbowing the catman in the ribs.

"Yow!" The catman let go.

Summer stumbled forward, hit a wall and turned to face the attacker. "I'm only interested in buying a little Zombium."

"Groutcrap." From under his neosilk windcheater he tugged a wicked knife.

Summer edged toward a window. "You folks don't have a very winning sales technique."

"Quit trying to con us."

Pivoting, Summer took a run at the window he'd picked. He hit it hard with both arms shielding his head. The glaz cracked, sending shards into the gathering darkness as he went sailing out in their wake

It was a shade less than ten feet to the beach. Summer landed on the sand on a knee and an elbow.

He rolled toward the sea, hitting the spray at the same instant that the catman's thrown knife dug into the sand at the spot where he'd landed.

Tugging at his stungun, he scrambled upright.

Zzzzzzzzzannnnnnnaggggg!

The catman had come leaping through the window.

In midair a thin beam of glowing red light had hit his chest. He suddenly burst into flame, from toe to head. The roar of the intensely orange fire drowned out nearly all of his screams.

Only a bundle of black ashes hit the sand. The ashes broke, scattered, mixed with the lapping surf.

"Don't bother to say thanks, pappy." Scoop was crossing the darkening beach toward him.

"What the hell did you do?"

"Saved your damn life, nurfhead." The customized cambot held up the middle finger of his left hand. "Using one of my built-in weapons to—"

"Why didn't you just stun the guy?"

"Looked as though he was going to do you in."

"Stunning would've prevented that." Summer walked over to the remains, watched the sea spill across the ashes. "Then I could've asked him questions when he came to."

"If you were still alive to ask them, clucko."

Summer said, "You're not even supposed to be here."

The robot said, "A good thing Vicky told me to tail you. She was fearful you'd dodder into a mess and need me to—"

"I don't need anybody to slaughter my sources of—"

"Knock it off, Summer. I made a decision and it's over," cut in the machine. "Do you want me to help you up the path back to—"

"What I want you to do is accompany me to the

ships' Security Police," Summer said evenly. "We'll try to explain why my damned cambot is murdering people."

"I'm not *your* anything, buddy boy. Keep in mind that—"

"Move," suggested Summer.

11

The Chief Forensic Medic was a plump, green-skinned humanoid. "My, my," he said, reading the strip of faxpaper that was clicking out of the chrome-plated scannerbox on his long, cluttered work table. "The victim—"

"Alleged victim," corrected Scoop. "You bozos haven't proved a—"

"Hush," Summer advised him.

"Button it," added the lean, crewcut catman who'd introduced himself as Inspector Doan of the Security Police. "Go on, doc."

"My, my," repeated Dr/2 Floyfloy. "The alleged victim had—"

"You don't have to say alleged victim for cripe sake," cut in Doan. "This pile of hardware doesn't have any authority so far as—"

"Think again, hotshot," said the camera robot. "You just better brush up on the Laws of Robotics before . . . awk!"

Summer had reached into the mechanical man's armpit and shut him off. "Let's continue."

"My, my," said Dr/2 Floyfloy with a chuckle, "the victim, alleged or otherwise, enjoyed his last meal at 4:45 PM. He opened with a delicate cold spinach soup —Venusian-style—then a hearty grout stroganoff, a henkelroot quiche and for desert a subtle frangipan gateau done in Hellquad style with a side—"

"I don't want a goshdarn menu," said Doan, rubbing a paw across his close-cropped fur. "Tell me who the guy was."

"I always think that what we eat is a key to our whole and entire—"

"ID him, doc."

"Yes, to be sure." He lifted the lid of the plaz shoebox that rested amidst the jumble of equipment. He scooped out another scoop of ashes. "I might mention again, inspector, that your habit of bringing me people's last remains in shoeboxes often interferes with my analysis. Need I remind you of the time last autumn that the explosion victim was mislabeled as a long-distance runner because you—"

"Tell me who Summer and his 'bot iced."

"Actually," said Summer, watching the green doctor shake the scooper of ashes into a chrome funnel atop another scannerbox, "this cambot doesn't belong to me at—"

"Cork it, Summer."

"See?" Dr/2 Floyfloy indicating the faxpaper starting to stutter out of the box side. "It's suggesting he was a softshoe salesman from . . . Ah, no. Back on the track now. Catman. Five-foot-eleven. Age, thirty-nine. Hobbies, crewel embroidery and tapdancing—well, I wouldn't bet on that last one. Interesting, though, that embroidery. You don't often find assassins who relax by—"

"Alleged assassins," said Doan. "We still don't know what these three were doing on the Malibu Deck."

The doctor touched a red dot of a button on the machine's glittering side. "Now let's get a specific ID by crosshatching with Central Personnel . . . Yes, fine. Here it is. Name is Polonius Watt-Evans. Employed as Best Boy on the *Hollywood II* production of *Haunted Mansions*. Has been aboard for eleven months and—"

"Damn." Doan poked Summer's arm just above the elbow. "Tell me again why you went to meet this Watt-Evans guy."

"I have a reputation for being interested in scandal and—"

"Yeah, I know that. I saw that biased vidreport you did last year about police brutality and it made me so mad I wanted to bust you in the—"

"This guy, without mentioning his name, sent me word he had some gossip to sell. Something to do with *Galaxy Jane*.

"And where does Jukebox Charlie fit in? You were spotted entering his joint."

"I like polkas and he's well-stocked with the latest—"

"Charlie's taken a powder, done a scamola. Did you know that, Summer?"

"Nope, I didn't. But since there's no way to leave the *Hollywood II* until it docks tomorrow on Murdstone, you—"

"Hell, there's a dozen places he can hole up on this damn crate," said Doan. "Okay, keep talking."

"All I know," said Summer, "is the catman jumped me soon as I stepped into that boat house."

"What'd he say?"

"Not a damn thing."

"Just grabbed you and tried to kill you?"

"That was sure my impression," said Summer. "My cambot got excited when he saw Watt-Evans coming for me with a knife. He shot him."

"Turned the poor lout into soot." He gave a muffled snap of his furry fingers to indicate the swiftness of the catman's going. "Okay, Summer, now you tell me if you're reporting on drugs or just using them."

"Beg pardon?"

"Watt-Evans was, I'm damn near certain, peddling serious drugs."

"Can you prove that?"

"If I could've, he'd be in the hoosegow now instead of a shoebox," answered the inspector.

"What about Jukebox Charlie?"

"A very, as you pointed out, musical fella."

"Is he on your suspect list, too?"

"That has just about nothing to do with what you're supposed to be—"

"Yipes!" A human SP sergeant came through the crime lab door backward. "You oughtn't to come in here, miss, because—"

"The heck I oughtn't." Vicky pushed him aside, came striding over to the work bench. "What's the darn idea of arresting my colleague and my equipment? This is an out and . . . Oh, hello, Norby."

Inspector Doan gave a slight negative shake of his head. "Evening, Victoria."

She was scrutinizing Summer, frowning over his mussed-up condition. "Did they rough you up? I know Norby has a degree in Persuasive Interrogation and . . . Scoop! What the dickens is wrong with you?" She'd noticed the robot was standing rigid, staring straight ahead blankly. She thumped his metal chest a few times, tapped his side. "He's dead, Jack. What—"

"Only sleeping," Summer assured her. "We shut him off so he wouldn't heckle the proceed—"

"Doesn't that violate his rights? What I mean is, how

can he exercise his inalienable right to speak up if—''

''Victoria,'' said Inspector Doan, ''are you associated with these two lunks in some—''

''You bet your britches I am.'' She faced him, hands on hips. ''And I want to make darn sure you aren't using police brutality on them. I know all about that sort of thing, and I even saw a vidreport about it on our NewzNet service last year—''

''That's what I was getting at about your irresponsible journalism, Summer,'' said the security cop. ''You influence the gullible viewer with—''

''I'm not exactly gullible, Norby,'' said Vicky, her anger and annoyance causing her to breathe exclusively through her mouth. ''As a dear and longtime friend of my father, I think you know me better than—''

''Victoria, a guy's been killed and—''

''Who?''

''Polonius Watt-Evans,'' said Dr/2 Floyfloy, lifting the shoebox and rattling it. A dark swirl of ashes puffed up free of the box.

''That's him in that dippy box?''

''All that remains.''

Vicky shook her head. ''I can't say I think much of the way you treat the—''

''Summer here claims your 'bot knocked him off,'' Doan told her.

''Scoop? No, that isn't possible. What I mean is, he's the most gentle of—''

''Vicky,'' cut in Summer, ''don't try to convince the inspector Scoop couldn't do it. Because I'm the only one who was around at the time.''

She glanced from him to the frozen robot. ''Neither one of you is a killer.'' She made an exasperated noise. ''Honestly, Norby, you have only to look into their eyes to . . . well, right now Scoop's eyes are a little dopey-looking, but usually he's got honesty and—''

''But this gadget man of yours does have deadly weapons built into him, doesn't he?''

"He does, sure. He's customized and when my father and I bought him, we decided to get the best extras available. A young woman who's chosen a career in journalism and who intends to travel to some of the sinkholes of the universe is going to need a robot who can handle most any—"

"Tell you what," said Doan as he gave his crewcut fur another nervous rubbing. "You and Summer can depart now. Doc and I want to run a few tests on your pal Scoop before we send him back to you with—"

"You're not going to get him all bunged up?"

"Nothing like that, child," said the green doctor, chuckling amiably.

"I don't want you sending him back to me in a shoebox."

"No, no, to be sure. We simply have to test his finger to see if it was indeed the one used to shuffle Watt-Evans off this mortal—"

"Gee, I really hate to leave Scoop all alone in this dingy lab while you—"

"Nevertheless, she'll do it," said Summer, taking her by the arm. "We'll see you later, inspector."

"That you will. Especially you, Summer."

12

Vicky's elbows tapped the table top as she leaned toward Summer. "I'm really nonplussed," she admitted. "What I mean is, what the heck is going on?"

He lifted his glass of sparkling water, took a drink. "Somebody wants to kill me," he said, "or at least slow me up considerably."

"That means we really are on to something." Sighing, she shook her head. "Except I don't have any idea what it is." The bite she took out of her bacon, lettuce, and tomato sandwich was unenthusiastic.

From behind the counter of the diner Bugeye called, "What's the matter with youse, honey? G'wan, chow down."

"Things on my mind." She took one more bite.

"It's that sourpuss youse hang around with," observed the green-toned cyclops. "Guy doesn't even want a plate of baked beans or a hunk of rhubarb pie. Rhubarb pie that we only get teleported in from the Earth System once a month if that."

"Bugeye," said Summer, "I'll have a piece of pie."

"Well sir, what do youse know?" He straightened his chefhat, rubbed at his chin, scratched his left buttock and tugged his apron smoother. "Plain or a la mode?"

"Plain."

"Why don't youse go whole hog, cheapskate?"

"Okay, two scoops."

Vicky lowered her voice. "Who sent that cat-man . . ." She shivered, hugging herself. "It's going to take me a little more time to get used to seeing what's left of people. What was his name . . . Watt-Evans?"

Summer nodded. "I may be able to backtrack on him," he told her. "Talk to my original contact and—"

"Did he really try to kill you?"

"He had a knife. Could be he just wanted to scare me some."

She said, "Another thing I don't exactly understand is how Scoop could kill anyone."

Summer watched her face as he asked, "What did you tell him to do?"

"What do you mean?"

"You instructed him to follow me and what else?"

"Jack, I never told Scoop to track you," she said. "That's not how I—"

"Okay, you've worked with him before. How independent is he?"

"Scoop's just a robot. He's supposed to do what's in my best—"

"One rhubarb pie a la mode." Bugeye bowed to place the dish in front of Summer. "Allow me to point out to youse, friend, that the bottom-most scoop of ice cream is heavenly hash, whereas the topper is tutti-frutti."

"And that's coconut atop the ice cream?"

"Mostly."

"Mostly?"

"I'll be brutally candid with youse and admit that now and again the ceiling plaster, in small quantities, mind youse, flakes and falls from aloft to bedeck whatever—"

"You ought to put in a plaz ceiling," advised Vicky.

"Not authentic for an Earth-style bistro," Bugeye explained. "The way youse can tell the plaster from the coconut is it's crunchier. The plaster is. And not quite so sweet." Winking his single orb at the young woman, he took his leave.

Vicky reached across with her fork to poke at the upper ball of ice cream. "That's plaster right there . . . Got it."

"When you were working with Scoop before, did he go off on his own without—"

"Actually, you know, I've only had him a few weeks," she replied. "Never took him along on a real assignment before. What I mean is, this is sort of his maiden voyage."

"After Doan goes over him," said Summer, "I better check him."

"Scoop is loyal to me *and* you. That's his nature, and it's in the warranty."

"Even so."

"But he saved your life, as I understand the setup. So why are—"

"He didn't have to kill the catman."

"He's been designed to make the best decision every single time. Therefore, he must've assumed that killing that—"

"Maybe."

"You're suspicious of everybody. I suppose that's the way I ought to be."

"Wouldn't hurt."

"Still, though, you weren't so suspicious that you avoided walking right smack into a trap so the catman could—"

"I walked in assuming it was a trap. If Scoop hadn't come clomping into the—"

"That's risky. Using yourself as bait."

Summer asked her, "How long have you known Inspector Doan?"

"Norby? Oh, it must be . . . oops, there's another fleck of plaster." She reached across again. "Norbert Doan used to be on the security staff of NewzNet. That was about five years ago and I got to know him then. My father used him occasionally for special— Do you suspect him of something shady?"

"Nope. It's only that you're the only person I know who can get by with calling him Norby," he answered. "I was curious."

"He's sort of an old friend is why. Although I think

he's being sort of dippy in this particular—"

"What's the matter with the pie?" Bugeye wanted to know.

"Nothing at all." Summer took a bite.

Climbing out of the whirlbath, Summer stepped into the dryer alcove and touched the *medium warm* button.

"Could somebody have taken over Scoop?" he asked himself while the warm air nozzles huffed at him. "Then why not kill me instead of the catman?"

Maybe they figured that was too risky. Murdering a NewzNet reporter, even one who was fast approaching middle age, would draw a hell of a lot of attention to the *Hollywood II*. Simpler to get rid of the source of information.

"But why send the catman to kill me in the first place then?"

He wasn't supposed to kill you probably. Just scare you off. When it looked like you might outfox him and get to question him, he was erased.

"Meaning Scoop has to be in on . . ."

Frowning, Summer shut off the drying unit.

He stepped clear of it, listening.

There came the noise again. Something scratching on the outside door of his cabin.

Putting on a terrirobe, he left the bathroom to cross to the door of the compartment.

A clawed hand was apparently scraping at the neowood paneling.

After taking a stungun from his robe pocket, he eased the door open.

Ezra Zilber was out in the corridor. His fur was standing on end, his staring eyes had a milky cast and his raised right arm was contorted. "Terribly . . . important . . ."

"Was just going to come looking for you," said Summer. "What the hell's wrong with you?"

"Overdose . . . Zombium."

Summer took the catman by the arm and brought him into his cabin. "Who gave it to you?"

"They . . ." Zilber's arms dropped to his side. His breathing grew more shallow, his eyes dulled.

"C'mon. Who?" Summer tightened his grip on the informer's arm.

". . . listen . . . dreadfully . . . important . . ."

"What is?"

"Tin . . ." gasped the catman, struggling to get the words out. ". . . Mahatma . . . isn't only . . ." His mouth dropped open, he ceased to speak.

"Zilber?"

The trance had taken over. The catman was at rigid attention, gazing blankly.

"Damn." Summer backed away from him.

"Geeze, what'd you do to this one?" Inspector Doan was in the doorway, scowling.

13

The inspector was prowling the cabin, opening closets, poking into cubicles, pausing to scowl at Summer and the stupefied Zilber. "Why do I get the impression you're groutshitting me?"

Summer shrugged one shoulder and sat on the edge of the tin slingchair. "Probably has something to do with your restless and inquiring mind."

Doan halted in the middle of the carpet, tugged a small cluster of wire and metal from his pocket. "Know what this is?" He flipped it toward Summer.

Catching the gadget, he scrutinized it. "Parasite control," he said. "Homemade. You find this planted in Scoop?"

Tapping the side of his furry head, Inspector Doan replied, "Planted inside his coco."

"Any idea by whom?"

"You're going to provide that info."

Summer grinned. "No idea," he said. "Unless the outfit that customized him for Victoria Nugent decided to—"

"There's another thing I don't get. How come they let a sweet and innocent, though moderately loony, kid like her travel to the wilds of Murdstone with an unreliable reprobate like—"

"You're letting your personal feelings cloud your judgement," Summer told him. "I'm a damn good journalist and she'll learn many a valuable lesson by working shoulder to shoulder with—"

"Okay, okay." He pointed a furry forefinger. "Knock off the mannyfranny. Just tell me what you're really covering for NewzNet."

"Told you already. We're doing a lighthearted report on the making of *Galaxy Jane.*"

"G'wan. They don't waste muckrakers like you on candyapple jobs like that," Doan asserted. "What you're really interested in is Zombium smuggling and trading."

"What Zombium smuggling and trading?"

Doan took a swing, punching Zilber on the arm. "You think maybe this clunk is just sleepwalking? He's zombed to the eyeballs."

"Seems like that's a Security Police problem."

"You know the size of my staff? You know how tough it is to lean on some of the important—"

"Is Zilber involved in smuggling or selling the stuff?"

"Didn't think so until now. I didn't have a damn thing on him."

"Who is involved then in—"

"That's my business."

"Right," agreed Summer. "I shouldn't even be asking you about all this. Excuse it."

After giving the entranced Zilber another punch, Doan asked, "Why'd this nance come calling?"

"Don't know."

"You were talking to him at the cocktail party last night."

"He was trying to interest us in doing an interview with him."

"And he came here tonight to ask again?"

"He didn't say."

Doan rubbed at his crewcut fur. "This guy's fighting against going into a trance, struggling to keep his wits about him before he conks out," he said. "He makes a terrific effort to see you before the Zombium overcomes him. And all of that is just so he can get himself a little publicity, huh?"

"A mention on NewzNet gets you known all across the universe."

Doan snorted, crossed over, snatched the parasite gadget from Summer's hand. "You're a real pain in the toke."

"You're not the first to notice."

"Before you . . . what?"

Someone had tapped on the door. "It's I, Dr. Gummox," called the lizard physician. "You got a sick man in there? Yes? No?"

"Yeah." Doan yanked the door open. "Take charge of this swish, doc. Stick him in the Infirmary, run some tests. I want to be damn sure what did this to him."

Crossing the threshold the doctor nodded at Summer. "How are *you* this evening, Mr. Summer? Fit as a fiddle? Yes? No?"

Summer said, "I'm fine. Whatever Zilber took, he took elsewhere."

"Ah, then this wasn't a friendly little drug orgy, eh?" He adjusted his neosilk lounging robe, then made a circuit of the stiff-standing Zilber. He sniffed, touched, frowned. "This foolish fellow has ingested a massive dose of Zombium."

"Make sure. And try to find out where he got it." Doan stomped into the corridor. "We'll keep in touch, Summer." He went hurrying away.

"Ah, this isn't good for my finances," confided the physician forlornly.

"How so?" asked Summer.

"The information I was planning to sell your network," Gummox replied. "It was that I suspected this gentleman of being involved with Zombium."

Summer stepped out of the twilight into the Club Troc.

Two pale young men were the only customers. One had a neowood stake protruding from a very believable wound in his chest.

"Sir," the one without the stake said to the passing Summer, "do we upset or otherwise unsettle you?"

"Not much, no."

"See?" the actor said in the direction of the bartender. "After a long, grueling day working on *Haunted Mansions*, we didn't feel like getting our makeup off before—"

"Do you know Ezra Zilber?" Summer wended his way through small floating tables to them.

"Not well."

"Not at all, in fact," said the one who was made up to look impaled. "And if you're looking for that sort of companionship, sir, let me point out that our delicacy and frailness is due almost entirely to—"

"Was Zilber on the set today?" He gave them a bleak grin.

"No."

"He was sick."

Nodding, Summer made his way to the bar. "Where's Thrice?"

"Who?" The bartender on duty was a husky hairless humanoid. He was stripped to the waist, decorated with intricate tattoos.

"Thrice Obelisky."

"You mean Five Times?"

"Five?"

"He fell heir to a fortune, so I hear. Spent some of the windfall on ladies of the night. Hence the name change."

"Inherited money out here in the vast reaches of space?"

"It was teleported in, so I hear." He extended an illustrated hand across the ebony bar. "I'm Holy Pictures Hogan. Care to hazard a guess as to how I got my nickname?"

After shaking hands, he said, "Those tattoos must have some religious significance."

"They surely do. Don't you recognize St. Bud in the various depictions?"

Summer scanned Hogan's broad illuminated chest. "Right, yes. St. Bud, founder of the Church of Fundamental Bicyclism. Should've realized that the moment I noticed that his bicycle had a halo over the handlebars."

"Blessed Bicycle," corrected the bartender, bowing his head on the words and affording a brief glimpse of the religious scene etched on his bare scalp. "You have to call it the Blessed Bicycle and dip the coco while so doing."

"Sure, what's a religion without ritual," said Summer. "Listen, I'm anxious to talk to—"

"Most of the illustrations that cover my body from

tip to toe depict the various near-martyrdoms that St. Bud suffered as he peddled the Blessed Bicycle across the length and breadth of the planet Murdstone to spread the holy word about Fundamental Bicyclism."

"I see him getting beaned with a brick there on your stomach. Now, about Five Times. Where can—"

"You have to say Sacred Brickbat, bow your head twice and make a little zigzag in the air with your left hand," explained Hogan, demonstrating the proper ritual. "What was it you were asking?"

"Anxious to talk to Five Times," explained Summer. "So if you can tell me where to—"

"He's retired from the saloon trade altogether."

"As a result of his sudden inheritance. Okay, where'd he retire to?"

"That's a poser," acknowledged the illuminated bartender. "His exit from the Club Troc, so I hear, was a rapid one. There was also an exchange of words with management."

Summer said, "If you hear from him, mention that Jack Summer is looking for him."

"Not Jack Summer the interplanetary muckraker and ace investigative reporter?"

"That's me."

"Well, it's been a pleasure to meet you, and share my religious iconography with you."

The two bit players from *Haunted Mansions* were arguing when Summer went by them on his way out.

". . . am I supposed to know you're getting sick?"

"Can't you tell by looking at me?"

"Looking at you, I'd figure you were dead. That makeup . . ."

Summer walked along through the endless dusk of the Sunset Strip Deck, passing a delicatessen, a saloon, an alley and another saloon.

He slowed, stopped. Turning around, he backtracked to the alley mouth and reached into its shadows. "This is not a wise course of action for you, Vicky," he said, tugging her out into the open.

"I was sort of following you."

"I surmised."

The blond young woman said, "Right now, if you must know, I am not feeling too darn zippy."

"Any specific reason?" He offered his arm.

She took hold and they commenced walking. "Well, I'm sort of frightened."

"Okay, when we reach Murdstone tomorrow, you can book passage back to—"

"Not that frightened," she said. "I'm sticking with this, but . . . did you know somebody took over control of Scoop with a parasite?"

"Doan informed me, yes." They reached an elevator. "Care to take a walk along the beach?"

"I'd like that."

The door whispered open.

"Sunlit beach?" Summer asked as they entered the yellow cubicle. "Or do you prefer moonlight?"

"Moonlight."

He pushed the button for the Laguna Deck.

Vicky was walking barefoot across the dark sand. "You think Zilber is a Zombium addict?"

"Nope."

"Then Dr. Gumdropz is—"

"Gummox." Summer had kept his boots on. "He's lying."

"Scared?"

"More than likely."

"Lot of that going around."

"They gave Zilber an overdose to keep him quiet. That no doubt impressed the good doctor."

She shivered, hugging herself and looking out across the believable moonlit sea. "Zilber must've had something darn important to tell you."

"That's Doan's theory."

"It could still be true. Even Norby is smart sometimes."

Summer said, "Not smart enough to nab the smugglers."

She kicked at the sand with her toes. "So what could Zilber know?"

"He might've found out who's heading the Zombium operation," replied Summer. "Might've found out how exactly they're smuggling the stuff."

"Did he manage to say anything to you?"

"A few words."

"Just babbling you mean?"

"Maybe babbling, maybe a clue to something."

"But you're not going to confide in me?"

"Not yet, no."

Vicky sighed. "It was Scoop, you know, who had his darn brain taken over," she said, stopping and looking seaward again. "I don't happen to be under the control of forces who—"

"All I've got right at the moment is some notions."

"You could share them. What I mean is, when you don't trust me, I don't feel like I'm an equal partner in this."

"You're not."

Her shoulders slumped. "I wish you hadn't said that. Makes it less easy to ask you what I was going to ask you."

"Which was?"

"Well, could you put your arms around me and hug me for a minute? That usually helps cheer me up when I'm glum and uneasy. Nothing romantic, but when somebody I feel is stronger and possibly wiser than—"

"Just keep in mind I don't do this for all my partners." He, gently, took hold of Vicky.

14

"You ought," suggested Summer to Scoop, "to be capturing all this on vidfilm."

"Nuts to you," replied the camera robot.

"Fellows," said Vicki, "stop this quibbling."

They were moving slowly through the crowded main lobby of the spaceport. The lavender-tinted glaz walls afforded a view of a hot, hazy afternoon on the outskirts of the capital city of Pegada Territory.

Near the arched gate to the Luggage Retrieval Facility nearly a hundred excited young females—catgirls, toadgirls, lizardgirls, humanoids—were screaming, sighing, swooning, waving flashing glosigns that declared their unbounded admiration for Francis X. Yoe. Some of them, in their enthusiastic hopping and fluttering, had knocked over the platform belonging to the Fairplay For Greenies Committee. Faxpaper leaflets demanding return of tribal lands and green men in two-piece worksuits were sprawled on the floor, entangled with youthful feet and legs. An elderly birdwoman, whose placard proclaimed her a member of the Senior Citizens Harlan Grzyb Fan Club, was trying to fight her way through the zealous Yoe admirers by swinging out with her plexiglaz crutch.

Summer caught Vicky's arm in time to keep her from colliding with the tail end of a marching group whose banners identified them as the Mothers Against Piracy.

"At least," she said, "I don't see any of your creditors around."

"We only just set down on the planet, angelcake," reminded Scoop. "The alimony fans'll no doubt come parading in at any—"

"Mr. Summer, Mr. Summer." Nudging aside an

obese toadwoman who was wearing a large tri-op Grannies For Grzyb badge, the incredibly beautiful Public Relations android from the *Hollywood II* threw herself gracefully into his path. "Thank St. Bud I found you. What with all the confusion of docking—"

"Why are you seeking me?"

"We have a special skyvan waiting outside," explained the gorgeous mechanism, "to take you and Miss Nugget directly to your guest cottages at the exciting *Galaxy Jane* locat—"

"Nugent," corrected Vicky with a frown.

Summer told the android, "Soon as we gather up our luggage, we'll—"

"Oh, that's all been taken care of. All you need do is follow me out to Skylot 3." After giving him a dazzling smile, she commenced forging her way through the crowds.

Scoop's camera lens swung toward her backside and he started whirring. "Might as well pretend we're interested in some of this local color."

"Honestly," said Vicky, "you two fall for the most obvious sort of—"

"Holy crow, lady," complained a squatting green man. "You just now trod on a good dozen or more of my leaflets. These babies cost us ten trucentz apiece to—"

"My father uses a place that only charges four," she told him, allowing Summer to escort her out in the wake of the PR andy.

Just as they stepped out into the afternoon, thunder rumbled off in the thick woodlands beyond the spaceport. The sky was a sooty yellow and growing darker.

"What's that sticky smell?" inquired Vicky.

"Bananas." Summer pointed a thumb. "Yonder lies one of the Galactic Fruit Company's largest blue banana plantations."

"Blue's a silly color for a banana."

"Right over this way, Mr. Summer," called the

beautiful auburn-haired android. She was standing next to a hovering orangish skyvan. "Jump in and we'll go whisking away to the *Galaxy Jane* encampment."

Summer stood aside to allow Vicky to climb into the skyvan.

The toadman in the driveseat wore a glittering helmet and had the goggles down over his eyes.

"Step aside, pappy." Scoop shoved his way aboard.

"Hey, you there. Mr. Summer, hold on!" A wiry, bald man in his middle thirties was trotting across the pink-paved lot toward them. Three cameras dangled around his neck and he was zipping up the fly of his trousers as he came running over. "My name is Dogbert Kameradschaft and I'm with the *Pegada Shopping News*. If I might, I'd like to snap your picture for—"

"Geeze it, that's the skinhead!" shouted the helmeted pilot. "Let's scram."

"I do hope you'll some day forgive me." Smiling fetchingly, the android kneed Summer in the crotch, gave him an enthusiastic shove and leaped into the skyvan as it went rising swiftly upward.

Summer sat down, against his will, on the pink ground. Gazing skyward, he saw the door of the van slam shut as it went whisking away through the overcast afternoon.

"Allow me." The bald man's cameras clacked together when he bent to assist Summer to his feet.

"Was this a rescue attempt on your part, Palma?" He was watching the departing skyvan grow ever smaller.

"It was indeed," admitted Palma, brushing at his fly. "I arrived here early to reconnoiter and, unfortunately, got into a very intense discussion with a young lady who works for the Interplanetary Travelers Aid. Time fairly flew, as it's wont to do when you're enjoying yourself, and when we got up off the floor of her lost luggage storeroom it was past—"

"Meanwhile those goons've swiped Vicky Nugent."

"But for the delay I'd have saved you one and all," said Palma somewhat ruefully. "I am, by the way, continuing in my efforts to cure myself of my habit of dwelling on the components of the female form. Yet I can't help mentioning that the Nugent heiress is a mite lacking in the casagmo department. That andy on the other—"

"One who booted me in the privates, you mean?"

"That android, yes. She possessed a set of, admittedly spurious, but still very—"

"You knew about this plot in advance?"

"I did, which is why I rushed here like the wind to—"

"What were they planning to do? Kill us or—"

"Kidnapping is what's afoot, old chum. They just want to keep you folks quiet for a spell. So the understaffed Miss N's life is not in—"

"Explain to me, concisely, how in the hell you got involved in this mess?"

"Can't do it concisely," said Palma. "If you'll accompany me to an out of the way bistro, though, I'll explain what's been going on here on Murdstone while you've been vacationing in space."

"Dr. Voodoo?" said Summer.

"That's what they call the scum," Palma assured his longtime colleague. "Dr. Voodoo is by way of being the mastermind of the Zombium trade." He picked up his menu, which had *Sea Food Grotto* gloletterred across its cover.

"Before you order a full-course snack," said Summer, "explain to me why we don't just go report Vicky's kidnapping to the local law."

"Wouldn't do any good," said the bald photographer as he brushed at his fuzzy moustache. "The police and the feds in Pegada Territory, a substantial percentage anyway, are corrupt. And a certain amount of the corrupting's been done by Dr. Voodoo and associates. Fact is, old buddy, it was a cop who mentioned to me the spaceport pageantry that had been planned for you and yours."

"Maybe we ought to talk to this cop so—"

"That'd be tricky, since the gent is no longer among the living." Palma scanned the menu. "Everything they serve here comes right from the ocean."

"How'd your informative lawman happen to expire?"

"Official accounts claim he disintegrated an essential portion of his skull while cleaning his crowd control pistol." Palma gave a forlorn shrug. "Could be he was spotted gabbing with me in a waffle shop over in the Greenie—"

"Any idea where they'll take Vicky?"

After a careful look around the small, shadowy restaurant, Palma said, "The original plan was to transport you and Victoria to a ruined temple off in the Great Woodlands, some hundred or so miles from here. Now, since they noted me and mayhap know I'm privy to their scheme, the location might change." He patted the top of his bare head. "Actually I was rather handsomely disguised with a full head of wavy locks. The damn wig got entangled with the handle of a portmanteau in the lass' lost luggage—"

"How'd you find out about Dr. Voodoo?"

"Initially I came out to this less than nifty planet to do a simple picture feature on the Murdstone Film Festival for *Envy* magazine," Palma told him while trying to signal one of the yellow-slickered robot waiters. "That turned out to be livelier than expected, since a goodly portion of the cinema industry attendees rioted when the top award—the prestigious and aptly named Blue Banana—went not to the favorite but to *I Slept With a Watermelon II*. They tore up plush seats, bashed—"

"This narrative is eventually going to get to Zombium and Vicky?"

"You're losing your gusto. In days gone by you'd

have savored all the pithy detail I'm able to toss into—"

"Yup?" A rusty robot had lurched over to their booth, tipped his yellow rainhat and begun searching himself for his order pad. "Yup?"

"I'll maybe have the Catch of the Day."

"Naw, forget it." The waiter continued to frisk himself.

"You don't recommend it?"

"For a while there, mate, it looked like it was going to be Mysterious Sea Creature," explained the robot. "But then the dang sea monster ate our fishing smack and all hands."

Palma said, "That's unfortunate."

"Why not have flying salmon on toast? Much safer."

"I'll go along with that."

"And you, mate?" The rusty robot had given up his quest for the pad and was scribbling on the sleeve of his slicker with an electromarker.

"Glass of sparkling water."

"Naught else?"

"I ate on the spaceliner."

"Let us hope the sparkling water hasn't gone flat again." He tottered off toward the kitchen.

"We've worked together, Palma, off and on, for well over a decade," said Summer. "And no matter what planet we're on, no matter what portion of this vast universe, you always drag me to the most godforsaken restuarants in—"

"I'm a gourmet and you're not. Simple as that." The bald photographer set his menu aside. "At the aforementioned film festivities I chanced to meet an absolutely charming young lady whose mambos, each in its own way, had personalities of their own. There was Lefty, shy and withdrawn, who . . . Anyway, Jack, I was a mite chagrined to learn that this particular stunner wasn't a universally respected starlet nor even an accredited gossip for a major news service. Nay, she was instead an undercover op for the Barnum Drug Bureau.

Her name, by the way, is Taffeta Silverstream and—"

"It figures."

"Eh?" He cupped a hand to his ear.

"All the women you get entangled with have impressive chests and dippy names like Taffeta or—"

"Dippy is a newish addition to your standard vocabulary."

"Vicky uses it."

Palma sat up, his frizzy moustache echoing his enlightened smile. "Ah, I comprehend now," he said. "That's why you're so grouchy, so agitated over this routine abduction and so uncharacteristically critical of my life and times. You're smitten with the fair Nugent heiress."

"She's a kid."

"A lass in her twenties is not too youthful for the likes of us," observed Palma. "Yep, I see it all. A typical shipboard romance—grizzled newzhound and demure multi-millionairess. They meet amidst—"

"Let's get on with your narrative."

"Taffeta is out here on Murdstone tracking down Dr. Voodoo," resumed the photographer. "Thus far nobody knows anything about Voodoo except his alias and the fact he heads up the Zombium trade."

"How'd you find out about my arrival and the plan to waylay us?"

"Sensing a yarn I could maybe peddle to *Galactic True Detective* or even our old alma mater *Muckrake*, I took to accompanying Taffy on her appointed rounds, armed with my trusty cameras. And that's how I came to learn you were expected, as well as what was in store for you," explained Palma. "Next to my loyalty to a provocative set of yonkers is my loyalty to my friends. I dropped everything to speed to your rescue."

Summer said, "Can you get us to this ruined temple where they may've taken Vicky?"

"We'll need a guide. A few well-placed queries ought—"

"I know somebody here in the capital who should be able to help us," said Summer. "Let's depart."

"You still haven't learned that nutrition is as important to what philosophers term 'the good life' as running around after—"

"Have them fix your flying salmon to go." Summer stood up.

So did Palma, though more slowly.

15

The heavy rain hit at the skycab as it attempted to climb to the landing deck atop the tallest tower in the capital city's business district. A strong wind was blowing across the early evening, slapping at the shivering cab. When bluish lightning crackled all around the struggling craft, the voxbox on the side of the automatic pilot commenced giggling hysterically.

"Tee hee . . . oh, my gosh . . . tee hee hee . . . good grief, what a ratty night . . . hee hee . . ."

The cab leveled off shy of its destination, began circling the penultimate floor of the towering glaz and plaz building.

"This vehicle doesn't inspire confidence," mentioned Palma, who was sharing the passenger seat uneasily.

"Should've done this earlier." Summer slipped a parasite control disc out of his pocket, stuck it to the dash and took over the piloting of their wobbly craft.

"I used to carry one of those dornicks," said the photographer as the skycab started climbing again through the storm. "Lost it, along with a handsome pair of white duck riding britches, when I had to execute a swift exit from a flying gondola near a space colony for nubile—"

"Better fasten your safety gear. Going to land this."

Thunder roared, the tower seemed to sway. When Summer set the skycab down on the dome-covered deck, the craft bounced twice, went sluicing thirty feet to the left, bounced once again and settled down.

Palma sank back in his seat and sighed. "I certainly enjoy the sound of rain pattering on a plaz roof." He sat for about a half a minute before starting to unfasten himself from the chair.

Before he was completely free the door on his side was yanked open.

"Blamsakes, Chavez, I didn't know you was hangin' around with Jack." A tanned, long-legged blond in a two-piece skirtsuit grabbed Palma enthusiastically and kissed him on the mouth.

"Finity," said Summer, "you're mistaking Palma for—"

"Dang, Chavez, what's wrong with you anyway?" Finity Kwark let go of the startled photographer and scrutinized him. "You shrunk 'bout a foot at least an' you sure don't smooch with that ol' zip an' . . . Heck, you ain't even Chavez."

"Would that I were."

"You sure do resemble him, bein' as cleanheaded as a meech melon an' sportin' that cute frizzly moustache," she said, tilting her head to one side as she continued to study him. "An', dangsakes, you even got that randy glow in your sexy ol' eyes. Shuxamighty, though, you're dinky. Who is you, anyways?"

"Palma," answered Palma in a voice not quite his own.

"Well sir, I'm darn sorry I hugged an' slobbered all over you, Mr. Palma," she apologized, touching at his cheek with her warm fingertips. "Thing of it is, I ain't seen Chavez since I quit the Interplan Law Service three years ago on account of my Cousin Turkey kicked off an' left me this here lucrative business. An' that's why you're here, ain't it?"

"Exactly," admitted Palma.

" 'Nother way I can tell you're littler than Chavez is you can't look eye to eye with me but just got to stare at the vicinity of my chest."

"That's mainly because I'm sitting down. Actually I'm rather on the tall side," the bald photographer said. "Relatively so."

"Blamsakes, don't be sorry for not bein' a giant." She touched his cheek again. "Lots of little ol' teenie-weenie folks are right nice anyhow. Fact is, my Cousin Turkey, rest his pretty near rotten soul, wasn't no taller than a wampus's backside. Course, you may come from a far'off planet where they got no idea what the heck a wampus is nor how high off the ground it's hind end is." She pressed her hands together and laughed. "Jack, you sure are patient, lettin' me go on babblin' to this cute little feller an' ignorin' you. We been friends ever since you helped me out that time back when I was residin' in Slum Gully on my native planet of Esmeralda an' we been penpals ever since even though I owe you about a dozen voxgrams at . . . Why the heck are you grinnin'?"

"Always do when I'm enjoying myself."

"Well sir, let's us get down to business," the blond said. "How can Safari Tours, Ltd. help you an' this condensed version of my ol' truelove?"

"Could we maybe go inside for that?" suggested Summer.

"Dangnation, I'm really gettin' goofy," Finity said, shaking her head. "Got no more manners than my Uncle Moot. Makin' you all sit out here on this storm-tossed spot. See, I got so all fired excited when you pix-phoned that I run right up here to wait for you, Jack. Climb out, the both of you, an' I'll take you down to my executive suite. I baked up a big batch of carob brownies an' brewed a whole big kettle of hot chocsub. Nothin' goes better on a spooky night than brownies an' something hot. How do you feel about that, Mr. Palma?"

"Hum?"

"Is he miffed, Jack, on account of I mistook him for another baldheaded feller?"

"What I think he's suffering from is awe," explained Summer as he climbed free of the cab.

"Really?" She laughed. "Well, for blamsakes."

Finity bent from the waist to tug a rolled map from off a low neowood shelf. "The Great Woodlands ain't a spot, I'll be frank with you, we get much call to guide tourists to," she said, unfurling the map. "Palma, honey, whyn't you move your mug of chocsub an' your little plate of brownies off that there coffee table so as I can spread this out."

"To hear is to obey." He scooped up the cup and the plate.

The rain was hitting hard at the wraparound viewin-dows, the frequent lighting turned the towers outside dazzling shades of electric blue.

She spread the map out, holding down its edges with a coaster and a ceramic snerg. "Tell you what, Jack, I'm goin' to have to escort you on this here trek myself," she said. "I don't trust none of my many wilderness guides, rough as they are, to handle it."

"We appreciate that." Summer sat on the arm of a lucite sofa to look down at the spread out map.

"Mostly, like I been tellin' you, we get wealthy ol'

offplanet visitors who want to play at huntin' an' explorin'," Finity said, kneeling down beside the floating table. "Murdstone's got more than its share of ruins, specially in Pegada Territory an' . . . Blamsakes, Palma, sit down an' relax yourself."

A heavy tin armchair came sliding over across the thermocarpet to nudge at his legs. He sat, muttering, "Much obliged."

When she shook her head, her blond hair brushed at her shoulders. "Dang, there I go showin' off again."

"Finity has a knack for telekinetic accomplishments," explained Summer.

Palma said, "I just reached that conclusion on my own." He sipped at his chocsub.

Touching the large map with a forefinger, Finity began to trace a course across it. "The first part of our journey—across forty or so miles of country—ain't likely to present any unusual hazards," she explained. "Just your ever' day brigands, wildmen, savage beasts, devilbats, dancin' bears, poisonous vipers, mean-minded—"

"Whoa there," cut in Palma as he wiped a crumb from his moustache, "mayhap you'd best explain how dancing bears can create a hazard. And, while so doing, fill us in on how they come to be residing in the forests beyond the capital."

"That I can surely do." She took a deep breath. " 'Bout sixty some years back a circusvan went an' got itself wrecked in them woods. Amongst the critters what escaped was six dancin' bears—four misters and two misses—an' they took to matin' an' replenishin' an' now they're a whole stewpot of bears. Hundred at least. Ever' blame one is a dancin' fool an' a natural born show-off. So you come barrelin' along a trail an'—wham!—there's three or four dozen bears waltzin' right in your path. Or they're maybe in the mood for jitter-buggin' an' they're throwin' each other around to beat the band, makin' progress on that road next to impossible."

Palma nodded. "I now comprehend the nature of the challenge."

She started her finger moving again. "This part of the forest's fairly safe an' there's a place called the Sylvan Oasis Inn where travelers can stop for a snack or—"

"Guy named Don Q. Capistrano still run that joint?" asked Summer.

Finity's faintly freckled nose wrinkled. "He surely does," she answered. "A big ol' sloppy birdman who can't keep his talons to himself."

"I'd like to stop and chat with him," said Summer.

"We can do that, I guess."

Palma assured her, "I'll see he minds his manners."

"It's mostly that I don't like to be hugged by anybody who's all-over feathers." She hunched her shoulders slightly. "Well now, after we pass Don Q., we then got to drive across the Gravespawn Swamp. Maybe you've heard tell of the place."

"Noted for its green men," said Palma.

"A nasty bunch an' they don't exactly take kindly to wayfarers," she said. "Though I don't pay any mind to them stories about them bein' cannibals. Anyways, we got to be mighty cautious crossin' Gravespawn. Course if it's as foggy an' misty as it usually is, they maybe won't even notice us." She crossed her fingers momentarily. "Let's hope they don't. An' that we don't stray into any dreamscapes."

"Which are?" asked Palma.

"Kind of a creepy part—well, heck, the whole dang swamp is creepy. Anyhow, folks tend to see odd things in these dreamscape patches. Hallucinations mostly, caused by special mists that ooze up out of the mucky ground thereabouts."

Summer said, "Wouldn't it be possible to fly over the whole area and land close to the ruins?"

"Nope, not no more," Finity said. "Part of this is designated a nature preserve an' on top of that, the Barnum Drug Bureau's persuaded the local governments to restrict flyin'. Only lawmen can take to the air. Supposed to help cut down on the Zombium smugglin', but it don't much, I don't think."

"What about the *Galaxy Jane* outfit?" Summer leaned to tap the map. "Their location headquarters is right here at the desert side of the Great Woodlands."

"From what I hear tell they went an' got special permission to fly their skyvans over the area," replied Finity. "Maybe you could pull strings an' get similar permission, but that'd take a few days an' you're in a hurry to get to where they're holdin' that poor heiress. With luck we can cover it on the ground in less than a day, Jack."

"Okay," he said. "How soon can we start?"

"I can have ever'thing ready by dawn."

"Fine. Meet you here?"

"Down on the ground level. That's where we got the landvans parked." She rose, gracefully, to her feet. "Don't you worry about extra weapons. I got a whole big stockpile of 'em." She held out her hand to Palma. "Been right nice meetin' up with you."

"The start," he informed her as he enthusiastically shook her hand, "of a deep and lasting relationship."

16

A flock of yellow birds went flickering by way up near the tree tops. They changed shades as they swooped out of stripes of morning sunlight and into stripes of shadow. Most of the trees had pale green bark and large spade-shaped leaves of bright orange. The brush, growing high and thick between the tall, straight trees, was a wild mixture of greens, purples and gold.

"Nifty," commented Palma, clicking off several more shots with one of his cameras. "I envision a nice exciting spread in *Galactic Geographic*."

"*I Was Eaten By Cannibals In The Wilds of Murdstone*," suggested Summer. He was seated in the rear passenger seat of the van cab.

"Scoff too much and I'll get somebody else to pen the picture captions." Leaning farther out the open window on his side of the rolling vehicle, the bald photographer took several more pictures. "What kind of moss is that dangling up on those branches, Fin?"

"Hum?" The tanned blond was in the driveseat, guiding the large, sturdy landvan along the forest trail.

"The purplish globs festooning the trees . . . What's it called?"

"Shux, that ain't moss at all. Those are nasty little critters known as puffers. They like to . . . pull in your pretty hairless head, honey!"

"Why ought I—"

Splattzzz!

A fist-size fuzzy purple ball had come hurtling down from above to splat against the windshield of the van.

"Them puffers are practical jokers and suicidal to boot," explained Finity, pushing a dash button that put forcescreens in operation at all the open windows.

After wiping a purple splotch from off the top of his head, Palma shot a few more pictures. Three more puffers plummeted down out of the intricacy of branches above. "Theirs seems an even less gratifying life than that of roving photog."

"Blamsakes, Palma, quit pretendin' you don't like your work. You're one of the most dedicatedest fellers I ever did see," Finity told him. "Heck, you took near to a hundred pictures of me whiles we was gettin' ready to leave this mornin'. That sure enough shows you love your job. Don't it, Jack?"

Summer nodded. "In most circles he's known for his devotion to his profession."

Finity touched another button on the neometal dash. The remains of the self-destructive puffers were whisked from the windshield. "I been thinkin' about what you fellers are up to," she said. "Not just rescuin' this poor lost rich girl, but pokin' into the Zombium smugglin' trade. It's awful dangerous."

"Ever hear of Dr. Voodoo?" asked Summer.

"Sure, he's mighty high up in the racket, an' just about nobody knows who he really is," she answered. "What he runs is the biggest, most successful Zombium operation. An' he's got a policy of wipin' out not only any drug agent but also any an' all competition."

"The gent's got rivals?" Palma was taking shots of a tree full of blue monkeys.

"Surely does," said Finity. "An' that's why, when we stop anywheres, you both got to strive not to get yourselves mistaken for Barnum Drug Bureau guys or Zombium smugglers. Lots of those kind of fellers get killed in these parts."

"How, dear child," inquired Palma, "could I be mistaken for else but the universally renowned lensman that I am? Fame is my passport, my safe conduct—"

"Dangnation, I bet ninety-two percent of the folks on Murdstone never heard of you, Palma."

Sighing, he let the camera he was holding drift down

to his lap. "Alas, that's probably true. Though I'd estimate the percentage at no more than eighty-nine."

"From what I've gathered since arriving," said Summer, "the territorial police don't much interfere with the Zombium industry."

"Blamsakes, would you throw a spanner in what was bringin' you a nice extra income? I'd guess ninety-four percent of the lawmen were on the take."

"More even than haven't heard of me," remarked Palma, as he raised his camera and gazed once more out his window.

Summer said, "And that's why nobody in the Pegada Territory government has plans to destroy the Zomba weed crops?"

"Heck, yes. That there's the biggest ol' money-bringin' crop hereabouts," replied Finity. "They'll just never go along with the Barnum Drug Bureau and dust the acres and acres of Zomba from the air with any poison that's gonna make the dang stuff shrivel up an' die."

"It occurs to me," put in Palma, "that the local government may not be any too fond of blokes who come muckraking into this mess. Has that thought occurred to you, old buddy?"

"More than once, yep."

"Should we run into any troublesome sorts, I'll pass myself off as a cheesecake photographer and you . . . Yoiks! A roadside accident."

They'd driven around a bend in the roadway. In a small clearing a landbus was lying on its side. It was painted a glowing crimson and had BIG TOUR! THE MODERN NOISE QUARTET emblazoned on its exterior in enormous studded letters. A lizardman, his spunglaz zootsuit tattered and bloody, was attempting to crawl out through a shattered window. A toadman, whose zootsuit was in even worse shape, was crouched in the high yellow grass and waving his instrument—a gold-plated bullhorn—feebly at them as they approached.

"Stop the vehicle," urged Palma. "We'll aid these lads and maybe get some nice shots for a piece I can sell to the *Intergalactic Auto Club News* or—"

"Jack, break out them stunguns from under your seat, honey," instructed Finity, speeding up the landvan.

"A trap?"

"Them's highwaymen," she replied as they went roaring by the seeming accident. "Ninnies actually. They tried this same dodge on me twice afore."

From the bullhorn the toad was tugging out a lazpistol.

"Let's discourage him." Summer raised a lazgun and aimed it.

Finity shut off the forcescreens. "Do it quick."

Zzzzzummmmmm!

Zzzzzzzummmmmmm!

Summer's first shot hit the toadman before he could get off a shot. The second caught the lizardman in the chest. He stiffened and dropped back inside the shadows of the tipped bus.

"Right nice marksmanship, Jack," said Finity.

"Aren't you going to compliment me on the nifty photos I got of the frumus?" asked Palma.

Finity laughed. "You're sort of an amusin' feller," she told him. "I almost like you."

"And that's after having known me for a mere day," Palma pointed out. "Wait until a week's dragged by."

"Does this bode well?" Palma stretched again, walked a few paces across the white gravel that was strewn on the parking lot of the Sylvan Oasis Inn, and nodded at the sprawling tile-roofed establishment.

The big vidboard over the wide porch flashed the message WELCOME INTERNATIONAL DIRTY WRESTLING CONVENTION! out into the gathering dusk.

"Even 'thout dirty rasslers this is a hellhole," commented Finity as she climbed, somewhat reluctantly, out of their parked landvan and commenced securing up. "But ol' Jack's bein' stubborn an' insists we—"

"You folks can wait in the van," said Summer. "I just want to chat with Don Q. for—"

"Heckamighty, I wouldn't let my worstmost enemy go traipsin' in there alone." She linked her arm in his. "C'mon, Palma, let's show 'em a united front."

The photographer took her other arm. They climbed the rickety steps. "I might be able to convince all and sundry I'm here to do a photo feature for *Home Beautiful.*"

"Let me do all the lying," requested Summer. "I know—"

The carved neowood door flapped open. Two lean catmen hurried out carrying something on a shrouded stretcher. They wore gloomy top hats, and had blackbands around the left sleeves of their gray frockcoats.

"You're too late for the services," said one.

"Get moving, Norman," said his associate.

"Hey, you ginks!" An apeman waiter rushed out and down the steps after the retreating pair. "You forgot part of him."

"My sort of hangout." Palma eased across the threshold.

"Anybody else come to play wrestling trivia with me?" demanded a huge humanoid cyborg who was sitting at a table near the bar. Instead of a right hand he sported a chainsaw. "Some of you schmucks must know more about oldtime wrestlers than me."

"That guy," said the uneasy birdman bartender, "seemed to know what he was talking about, Slice."

"Like hell. I know more about the career of Masked Murphy than anyone on this whole frapping planet."

The bartender polished a glass. "Thing of it is, Slice, that *was* Masked Murphy," he said. "Guy was here as the Guest of Honor for the—"

"He was old," pointed out Slice. "You get old and you get forgetful."

"Don't get mad now, but I got a hunch Don Q.'s going to be a mite ticked," said the bartender, gripping the edge of the bar with both feathery hands. "We got two hundred and some dedicated wrestling buffs signed up for the banquet in our Pastoral Room this evening and you go and butcher the G.O.H. just—"

"Hey, you schmucks what just come in." Slice rose up, gesturing at them with his chainsaw. "Any of you know a blasted thing about wrestling?"

"About what, sir?" Palma cupped his hand to his ear.

"Wrestling, you skin-headed little rammerjammer."

Frowning, Palma walked over to him. "I no longer take offense at slurs about my streamlined dome," he explained. "However, since I'm unfamiliar with the term rammerjammer, I'm not at all certain but what you haven't insulted me in a—"

"Course I have, you pecker-headed little putz." The chainsaw started growling. "And now I'm going to—"

"Slice." A few feathers popped free of the anxious bartender's head. "Don Q.'s going to be annoyed enough about your dismantling Masked Murphy. I wouldn't go—"

"Don't intrude." Slice warmed up his saw by cutting a spare neowood chair in half.

"Best thing for you to do," suggested Summer as he joined them, "is sit back down, Slice."

"What?" He raised his roaring chainsaw high. "You schmos think you can come into my favorite hangout and insult me and I'm going to let you?"

Summer grinned. "That's exactly what I think."

Slice snarled, eyes meeting Summer's. After about a half minute he dropped his glance, turned off his saw and sat down. "Well, since you're newcomers, I'll let you off this time."

Summer crossed to the bar. "I'd like to see Don Q."

"You can, you can," said the birdman. "Right down

that hallway to your left. Door that says Manager on it."

Finity came over to them. "Dangsakes," she said. "For awhile there I thought sure I'd be havin' to use my telek abilities."

Don Q. Capistrano steepled his feathery fingers, made a few thoughtful clucking sounds and leaned back in his desk chair. He watched the big ceiling fan spin fitfully for nearly a full minute. "Zombium you say?"

Summer was sitting closest to the obese birdman's wide rubberoid desk. "We're especially interested in a gent they call Dr. Voodoo."

Capistrano readjusted his gold-tasseled fez. "Have you folks ever heard of Fritch's Syndrome? A rare brain malady that causes selective forgetfulness," he said. "Thus far the only thing to cause even partial relief is—"

"I always pay for information."

"You do? I'd forgotten." He smoothed the coat of his rumpled three-piece white suit. "It takes one thousand trubux to goose my poor afflicted brain cells into action these days, Jack."

"Blamsakes," whispered Finity to Palma, "his whole entire brain ain't worth that."

"Five hundred," counted Summer, producing five 100-trudollar bills from inside his jacket.

The immense birdman stared at him. "What were we discussing? My mind tends to wander off a great deal since I contracted this dread—"

"Seven-fifty," said Summer, grinning. "No more."

Capistrano studied the pink and blue bills in Summer's hand. "It's all coming back to me now, Jack," he said, reaching a clawed hand for the cash.

"Give me a sample of your recovery." He held on to the money.

"Very well. Dr. Voodoo—and nobody knows for

certain who he is—controls the major Zombium processing and smuggling in the territory," Capistrano said. "There are two rival factions, much smaller."

Summer dropped the bills on the desk top. "What about the *Hollywood II*?"

The birdman scooped the money up, folded it neatly in half, tucked it into an inner pocket of his white jacket. "Tied in," he said. "But I'm not sure how."

"Does," asked Palma, "any of Dr. Voodoo's finished product pass through these parts?"

Glancing at the bald photographer, Capistrano said, "Voodoo transports it out some other way. Not on the ground."

"So how do you buy the stuff in these parts?"

"I don't deal in anything as rough as—"

"*If* you did," said Summer.

"I'd deal with one of his rivals. Most of Voodoo's product is for export to other planets."

"Who are these rivals?"

"Listen, Jack," the birdman said, "an interest in the workings of the Zombium trade isn't the safest occupation a journalist can have. Some of these lesser dealers have been known to rough up anybody they suspect of being a reporter or a BDB agent. So why not concentrate on Dr. Voodoo and forget—"

Zzzzzattttttzzzzz!

The neowood door to the private office ceased to be there.

While the ashes it had become were settling to the floor, three burly humanoids, thick with deadly weapons, came in.

"We don't like media snoops," announced the biggest and burliest.

17

"Allow me," said Palma, rising from his chair, "to clear up a misunderstanding. None of us, not a one, is affiliated with any known medium. On the contrary, we're dedicated archeologists intent on—"

"Park your arse, cleanhead," advised the leader of the trio of louts. "We recognized you immediately you entered the saloon as Palma, the galactically famed photographer."

"Well-known," added his colleague, letting his kil-rifle swing around until the barrel pointed at Palma's chest, "digger of dirt."

"This other gink," said the third well-armed intruder, "is no doubt Jack Summer, muckraking vid-journalist and noseyparker."

"We do," admitted Palma, "vaguely resemble those two lads. Fact is, we're often mistaken for them and that causes, let me tell you, a good deal of confusion and—"

"Didn't I tell you to sit?" The leader took hold of Palma's shoulder, forced him to reseat with a thump.

"Blamsakes," muttered Finity, anger growing. "That's just about all the hooroarin' I'm gonna put up with."

The three drugrunners made sudden trips up from the floor. Their weapons were jerked from them and then their thick heads thwacked the beams of the high ceiling.

"Holy crapola!" exclaimed the leader.

"Nifty." Palma took a few shots of the dangling trio overhead.

"Would you like to ask these three sodkickers some questions, Jack?"

Summer said, "Who do you guys work for?"

"Go weep in your chapeau, buster," said one of the louts that Finity was keeping suspended by exercising her considerable telek powers.

"We didn't bust in here to spill our secrets to media people."

"Dang, I was ahopin' you wasn't gonna be stubborn."

A fallen kilgun wooshed up from the carpet, flew right up to the ceiling and leveled off with its barrel touching the leader's head.

"Now you just better up an'—"

"Like hell. All I got to . . . Yow!" He'd attempted to snatch the floating pistol. Now he was suffering a severe hand cramp.

"C'mon and cooperate with Jack."

"Who do you work for?" he asked again.

"We're self-employed."

"Don't work for Dr. Voodoo?"

"That bastard? Naw, we're in competition with him," the leader said. "Hell, just yesterday some of his myrmidons tried to coldcock us in the Gravespawn Swamp."

"How'd that come about?" Palma moved to a new location for some further photos.

"We chanced to bump into 'em while they were transporting some bimbo and a snide robot to—"

"Whoa now," cut in Summer. "Was this a blond young woman?"

"Sorry I dubbed her a bimbo if she's a friend of—"

"Where was this?"

"In Gravespawn, like I told you."

"I want specifics. Do you know where they were taking her?"

"To the Haunted Caverns."

Summer glanced at Finity. "Know where they are?"

"Not exactly. I don't spend all that much time in the—"

"Where are they?" he asked the dangling lout.

"Geeze, you want I should draw you a goddamn map?"

"Good idea." Summer grinned.

Finity nodded. "Get busy."

A sheet of paper went floating up from Capistrano's desk top toward the leader's knobby right hand.

"She was a skinny sort of bim . . . young woman," he said, snatching the paper out of the air. "Didn't look to be worth all this—"

"A little more cartography," suggested Palma, "and less chitchat."

"I don't possess a pen."

"Here for dangsakes."

An electropen rose off the desk.

"Hey there, that's the very pen my Cousin Nick gave me when I graduated from Dismal Seepage Middle School," protested Capistrano, his tassel flipping when he shook his feathery head.

"He ain't gonna hurt it none. Are you?"

The leader caught the pen, started sketching. "You got to go careful through this stretch of country or—"

"Why warn 'em, Rosco?" Let 'em have a rough-arse time so's—"

"Who's doing this frapping map? When I draw one up, my pride as a woodland scout is called into—"

"But why be cordial to a bunch what's humiliated us and . . . Ooof!"

Finity had caused the complainer's skull to bonk a neowood beam three times. "Quit all your dang bellyachin'."

"These little squiggles," explained the mapmaking lout, "represent palm trees. Whereas these zigzaggy ones are weeping willows and—"

"Speed it up," advised Summer.

"You go wandering into a dreamscape, buster, and you'll know why it's important to tell a palm from a . . . Geeze, the pen's out of fluid."

"That can't be," said the uneasy birdman. "There's a lifetime supply."

"Well, maybe it's the gravity way up here."

"Try this." Finity caused an autopencil to fly upward.

"Not going to look too neat, using a different—"

"Just draw," said Summer.

The leader resumed his sketching. "This circle's the greenie encampment. Voodoo's got a bunch of them guarding the caverns."

"How many?"

"Hundred men at least."

In another five minutes the map was finished. Finity moved it down to Summer.

Glancing over it, he nodded and put it away in a trouser pocket. "We can get on the road again."

"Um," said Capistrano hesitantly. "What about my pen?"

"Dangsakes, I plumb forgot."

After the electropen was back in his hand, the obese birdman tried it out on a memo pad. "That's a relief, it still functions."

Watching Summer cross to the doorless doorway, the leader inquired, "What about us?"

Bending gracefully from the waist, Finity was helping Palma gather up all the fallen weapons. "You'll come down when we're away and clear," she told them. "All this hardware you'll maybe find in the woods somewheres."

"Have a heart, lady. We—"

"Just hush up or there'll be lots more head thumpin' goin' on."

They stopped talking.

As Finity was crossing the barroom a snergtrapper made a wobbly lurch out of his chair and attempted to grab her. "Sweetie pie, let's you and me—"

"Hooey."

He, making a surprised wooshing noise, left the floor,

sailed around the murky room once and then slammed headfirst into the wall just below a stuffed grout head.

"I surely dislike grabbers," she confided in Palma.

18

Palma drummed his fingers on his camera. "One of my major regrets is that we have yet to see a single dancing bear," he said, watching the misty darkness the landvan was rolling through. "I know I could sell some pix of them to *Ballroom Dancing* or perhaps even *Vacationing Surgeon* or—"

"Could be they're sitting this one out." Summer was driving.

Finity occupied the seat beside him and was studying their handmade map. "Them critters are right smart," she said toward Palma in the backseat. "You ain't gonna find a one in Gravespawn Swamp."

The photographer asked, "How does this charming parcel of fetid real estate come by its charming name?"

"Well sir, now . . . Jack, you want to take the left-hand road when we get to the next fork. Well sir, now, there are all sorts of explanations. Not any of 'em specially cheerful."

The mist was growing thicker, seemed to be swallowing the beams of their headlights.

Finity reached out to touch a dash button. "We better use our sensors."

A small voxbox began to hum and a rectangular screen came to life. The road ahead, much less fog-bound than it actually was, appeared. ". . . watch out for that hole . . . little bit to the left . . . look out for that hopfrog . . . What's that? . . . Unk! . . . Somebody ran over a treecat . . ."

Palma said, "Those goons back at the inn might've been lying to us, Jack. That chart may just be a work of fancy."

"Dangsakes," said Finity, sitting up. "Glad you reminded me of them three hooligans, Palma honey. I clean forgot an' left 'em hangin' up near Don Q.'s ceiling." She closed her eyes briefly, concentrating. "There."

"That's some knack you have," said Palma.

"Ain't that much. You ought to see what some of my brothers could do."

"This sort of thing runs in your family?"

"Well, they weren't actual my kin at all. They just up and pretended they was," she replied. "They got hold of me when I was just a little bitty thing an' raised me in Slum Gully on the planet Esmeralda . . . Heck, but that's a whole other story."

". . . watch out for that rut . . . swing a little to the right or you'll hit that root . . . What are you stopping for?"

Summer had braked to a stop, was frowning out at the foggy swamp road in front of the van. "Much as I'd like to, I don't want to run into any of these alimony collectors who're all over the roadway."

"Billcollectors?" Palma squinted.

"Blamsakes, Jack, your eyesight sure ain't so hot. That's only just about a half dozen of my meanest brothers an' cousins," said Finity. "Dang, I wonder how they found me way off on this planet?"

"Folks, what say we cease all this kidding around,"

suggested Palma, "and invite that ladies' softball team in for a cup of chocsub? Wearing those skimpy costumes, they must be nearly chilled to the bone."

"Whatever's the matter? . . . road is perfectly clear . . . except for . . . um . . . a flattened snerg . . . Continue on your journey . . ."

Summer shut his eyes, shook his head vigorously. "Finity, we're in a dreamscape," he said. "Each of us is seeing a different thing."

"I didn't quite hear what you said, honey. What with my relatives makin' all that unseemly hooroar outside there."

"You're absolutely right, more's the pity." Palma put his hands over his face. "We're having hallucinations."

Finity said, "But accordin' to the map we're a good ten miles from any dreamscape."

"Nevertheless." Summer put the landvan in reverse. "Everybody concentrate on not seeing anything unusual and I'll get us to the crossroads."

". . . foolhardy . . . going backwards in the wrong direction . . . better go around that pit that's opening up—"

"Pit?" said Summer.

Less than ten seconds later the van sailed over the rim of the wide pit and fell a dozen feet down to the loamy ground below.

Palma untangled the straps of his cameras. "That was some pothole." He rubbed at the top of his head, gritted his teeth, began feeling at his arms and legs.

"Dangsakes, we went and drove right into a trap." Reaching over, she touched Summer's shoulder. "Did that drop jiggle you up something fierce?"

"I'm okay. You?"

"Chair and safety gear pretty much protected me," Finity answered. "I can use my telek knack to lift all of us out of this dang ol' hole. But it's gonna be maybe too much of a strain gettin' this landvan back up on the road."

Summer cautioned, "Don't use any of your powers yet."

"But, Jack honey, it's a lot easier than climbin' straight up a dirt wall an'—"

"My hunch is that the folks who set this trap will take us to Vicky and Scoop once they collect us."

"Well sir, that's right clever. And maybe a whole lot easier than tryin' to follow this sloppy map."

"The cheese in the rat trap of life," sighed Palma. "That seems to be my destiny."

"Once we're inside their hideaway," said Summer, "then you can elevate them and we'll take over."

Palma asked, "Do we just sit here and—"

Kathump! Thunk!

Something that sounded like booted feet, two or three pairs, had landed on top of the van.

A moment later a green man in robe and burnoose lowered himself into the gap between the driver's side of the trapped landvan and the dirt wall of the pit. He held a glowing lightrod in one hand, a kilgun in the other.

Another similarly garbed and equipped green man appeared on the other side of the trapped vehicle.

The first green man pointed at his gun with the beam of his lightrod, made a come-out gesture, smiled nastily, then repeated the come-out motion.

"First time I've ever played charades in a location like this," observed Palma.

"Okay, we're coming out." Summer held up his empty, weaponless hands.

There was a ladder of neometal and spunglaz rope dangling over the edge of the pit. When the three of them had climbed up onto the mossy ground, prodded and urged from behind by the pair of green men, they were confronted by a dapper apeman in a conservative three-piece gray bizsuit.

"For a limited time only," the apeman said, patting

the neohide attaché case he carried, "we're offering you the opportunity to surrender peaceably."

"Who're you working for?" asked Summer.

"We're not at liberty to . . . Well, bless Bess, if it isn't the gifted Finity Kwark."

"You know this guy, Fin?" asked Palma.

"Dangsakes, it's Salesman Sam. An' I was hopin' he didn't—"

"Can't have you using your sensational gifts on us, little lady."

Summer realized why she was hesitating. "Okay, you better go ahead and—"

Zzzzzzummmmmmm!

A stungun beam came flashing out of a small hole in the edge of the attaché case. It hit Finity beneath her left breast and, before she could use her telek power on the apeman, she stiffened and then fell against Palma.

19

Vicky Nugent's smile faded. "I guess this isn't a rescue after all," she said, noticing that Salesman Sam and an armed green man were coming into the cavern behind Summer.

"It started out as one," he told her. "How are you?"

"Miffed," she said as she crossed the rough plank

floor to him. "First they dragged me to some dippy ruins, then they decided to transfer me here to this cesspool of a location. And, you know, they've flummoxed up poor Scoop again. He's on their side now and even crustier than usual."

"Says you, sister." The camera robot was leaning, metallic arms folded, against the dark stone wall near the entrance to the large cavern. "I finally figured out what side my sudobread was butsubbed on, that's all. Try to make an escape, Summer, and I'll—"

"Scoop, you really are an awful disappointment," Vicky said. "Are these your friends coming in now, Jack? Yes, that must be Palma—what I mean is, he's bald and horny-looking *and* he's carrying a woman."

"Folks, you have here the opportunity of a lifetime," said the well-dressed apeman, the light from the floating yellow globe high above him causing the silvery fastenings of his attaché case to sparkle. "Yes, you'll be living here in rural surroundings that are the envy of all. A few choice locations remain and they can be yours. Should you try to relocate elsewhere, the consequences could be extremely dangerous."

"I'll frizzle the lot of them should they get cute," promised Scoop, whose eyes had a strange glow to them. "Been itching to use all my built-in weapons. And what might you be staring at, cueball?"

Palma answered, "We're colleagues, fellow lensman, and as members of that sacred brotherhood of—"

"Nertz," commented Scoop. "I wouldn't belong to any bunch that had a wall-eyed, bandy-legged skinhead like you in it."

Palma smiled beatifically and carried the unconscious Finity over to one of the neocanvas cots along the rear wall. "How long will she be out, Sam?"

"We guarantee a full night of deep and restful sleep."

"Do the same for you sometime, old buddy," muttered Palma, while covering the stunned blond with a plyoket.

Summer watched Salesman Sam. "How long are we going to be your guests?"

"Your enjoyable stay depends on several factors that are no concern of yours," he answered. "Since you've been much too unwise and curious about the activities of Dr. Voodoo, it was decided to keep you out of circulation until certain other events have transpired. Until then, make yourselves at home and allow me to wish you a pleasant good evening." He bowed and he and the green man backed to the entrance of the cavern. "Besides the talented Scoop, who'll remain on duty right here, a substantial number of guards are patrolling outside. Nice meeting you all." He moved out into the thick mist outside.

Taking hold of Summer's arm, Vicky pulled him closer to her. "Listen now, I'm on to something," she said softly, inclining her head very slightly toward a thick neowood door at the rear of the vast natural stone room. "They've got a lab in the next cave."

"To process Zombium?"

Vicky shook her head. "They're building android replicas of people," she said. "I got a good look in at a couple of them, Jack, and one is Flo Haypenny in her Galaxy Jane outfit."

The chubby green man chuckled, kissed his emerald fingertips and winked at the steaming stewpot he'd just placed on the rough-hewn round table. "You'll find it absolutely delicious, ladies and gents," he assured them as he dealt out plaz bowls.

Palma, resting on his elbows, eyed the contents and inquired, "Why is it glowing faintly?"

Tugging a loaf of gray bread from beneath his striped robe, the green man chuckled yet again. "That's a characteristic of firerats," he explained. "Technically the phenomenon is known as bioluminescence."

"Firerats would be rodents who glow like fireflies?" asked the photographer.

"You've grasped it." He dropped three plaz spoons and an equal number of forks near the greenly glowing pot. "Oh, and for those who, for whatever dietary reasons, don't eat firerats, this hearty ragout is also rich with potatoes, carrots and drumgoogles."

Palma was watching the faintly pulsing surface of the stew. "Drumgoogles are the ones with the abundance of little legs?"

"You've hit it," he said, backing toward the narrow entrance of the big cave. "Enjoy."

"This is the dippiest meal so far," commented Vicky, who was sitting next to Summer and across from Palma.

"We'll pretend to dig in." Summer spooned out a bowl of the glowing stew. "We can talk while Scoop thinks we're dining."

The cambot was still standing near the entry, arms folded and a look of disdain on his face.

"I'd like at least two drumgoogles in mine," requested Palma. "That way I can race them, one against the other."

"Why all the complaints? This food seems a couple notches better than what they serve in the places you usually haul me to."

"Could be it's the atmosphere that's making me gloomy."

Summers dished out a second bowl. "How much do you know about the layout here, Vicky?"

"Did you see any campfires when that wretched Salesman Sam brought you in?"

"Couple, off in the fog about five hundred yards away."

She said, "That's the green men's camp. I'd estimate there are between seventy-five and eighty of them in tentpods there. All men, no women or kids."

"How about transportation?"

"On the far side of the camp there's a clearing with maybe four or five landtrucks and one landcar."

"Meaning," said Palma, breaking a chunk of bread

off the loaf, "we have to get through or around a hundred armed rascals to swipe a getaway car."

"First we have to get by the guards," she said.

"How many?" asked Summer.

"Five at night usually, at least a couple more daytimes," she said. "And don't forget Scoop. He's the first obstacle to overcome."

"Sunk without a trace." Palma watched the bowl of stew he'd just dropped a piece of bread into. "Forgive me for waxing nostalgic, Jack, but do you recall that occasion when we were covering the skybridge collapse scandal out in the Trinidad System of planets?"

"Just thinking of the same thing."

"As part of our cover, we traveled with the Maximus Brothers Circus and I grew quite chummy with Princess Framboza, who was the proud owner of a set of casagmos that—"

"What's another of your yarns about some floozie with enormous breasts got to do—"

"The princess," explained Palma, "was a gifted hypnotist. And, under the spell of my considerable charms, revealed many of her secrets to me. None of which, I assure you, I have forgotten."

"You think you can hypnotize Salesman Sam and then a half dozen—"

"The fair princess didn't hypnotize people," said Palma. "Nay, nope and no. Her act was special. She hypnotized androids and robots."

Palma scratched the small of his back against the jagged stone wall of the cavern. "What a vista," he exclaimed enthusiastically, squinting out through the entryway at the midnight mist. "Fascinating how the swirling fog makes patterns that almost look like spectral spooks, shrouded spirits and other denizens of the nether world. I wouldn't be at all surprised if that's the reason they call this whole blessed swampland Gravespawn. Those ghostly—"

"Why don't you button your yap," suggested Scoop.

"Don't like to chat about graves and ghosts, eh, colleague? Reminds you of your own mortality no doubt. That's understand—"

"I don't have to worry about mortality, doubledome," the cambot told him. "I'm built for the ages. What say you toddle over to the cots and sack out like your halfwit cronies?"

"Takes me awhile to get used to sleeping in a new place," explained the photographer. "Hotels, skytels, caves. I'm usually restless for—"

"Then just go sit someplace."

Raising both hands to chest level, Palma stretched them out. "One of my hobbies is shadow pictures," he confided. "Not bunny rabbits, ducks, snergs and the like. More complex creations, ones that utilize all my digits in intricate ways. Watch my fingers, Scoop, old chum."

"One of them's glowing."

"That's a speck of firerat gravy I expect. Keep ogling. Note the way the thumb is ticking, ticking in exact time, I trust, with your central control mech. Fascinating, what? Ticking, ticking. Time passing and we're all of us that much closer to the great oblivion. Except, of course, those of us who are robots. That's right, concentrate. Watch my other mitt, too. Concentrate."

"This is really inane," murmured the robot, voice taking on a drone, "and yet . . . and yet . . ."

"Actually, what's happening is rather interesting," said Palma as his stubby fingers danced. "I'm taking control of your mechanical brain."

"By godfrey . . . you are at that . . ."

"Now, what I want you to do is trot along with me over to my cot," instructed Palma. "That's right, now sit down and let Jack remove the parasite control that's planted in your cabeza. Okay?"

". . . doubt it's in my own best interests . . . but I

guess I'll do it even so . . ." Stiffly, arms hanging at his sides, Scoop settled on the cot.

Summer rose up from his feigned sleep. "Very impressive," he told his longtime partner.

"You ought to see me when I do this with slot machines."

"I have."

"Ah, yes, I was forgetting the time the Venusian Mafia chased us through—"

"Let him get working," urged Vicky.

Using a plaz fork and a neometal hairpin, Summer deftly, and quickly, removed a portion of the robot's gleaming skull. "Simple enough control parasite they used," he said.

"Can you also modify his personality while you're in there?" Palma inquired.

"Here we go." Summer plucked a coin-sized gadget from off the mechanical man's brain and shut his head up. "Another homespun creation." He dropped the parasite in his pocket.

Vicky frowned. "Poor Scoop still looks sort of dippy."

Palma held his right hand in front of Scoop and snapped his fingers. "You're no longer under my spell."

"You put me in a strange position, skinhead," said Scoop. "I'm grateful for being restored to my natural efficient and amiable self, yet I truly cringe at the thought that I have to be grateful to you and your antiquated chum."

"That's quite enough sass," Vicky told him. "Customized or not, Scoop, you're going to have to start behaving in a much more cordial fashion."

"Angelcake, I'm a model of—"

"I want to look in the lab before we depart," said Summer. "Can you pick the lock and defuse the alarm system, Scoop?"

"Don't I have state-of-the-art equipment for just such a task built right into my person?" The cambot stood, walked to the lab door. "Piece of cake."

Three and a half minutes later they were all inside the next cavern.

It had neotile flooring, whitewashed stone walls and an array of low tables and considerable equipment. Stretched out on the off-white table closest to the door was a very lifelike android replica of Flo Haypenny. A Galaxy Jane space pirate costume was piled on the floor beside the table and the figure was unclothed.

Palma eased up to the table, thoughtful. "What's wrong with those yonkers?"

"This is not the time," said Vicky, "to indulge in your lowbrow breast fetish."

"You misinterpret, lass." He frowned at the figure. "They don't sit right."

"Well, that's because she's an andy and not—"

"Nope, the rest of her flesh sags the way it ought to when she's stretched out like this." Palma crouched, reached out and pinged the left breast. "Hollow."

"Be a nice place," said Summer, "to conceal something."

Palma gripped the breast, twisted. "Let's find out." He unscrewed it and tipped it over. "Lined with impervium."

"Meaning whatever you stashed inside it couldn't be spotted with ordinary detecting gear."

"Not the kind they use at most of the spaceports around the universe."

Vicky said, "You mean that's how they smuggle Zombium from planet to planet?"

"It's one way at least." Palma tapped the Flo Haypenny simulacrum on the knee. "This is hollow, too."

"This android," calculated Summer, "could hold at least 1,000,000 trudollars' worth of the stuff."

"And Dr. Voodoo, whoever he may be, could have

dozens of them. When they get ready to move a shipment, he subs a few andies for real actors and actresses and—wham!—the stuff is through customs and past the Barnum Drug Bureau. I mean, who's going to go up to somebody they think is the famed Flo Haypenny and unscrew one of her boobies?"

"You might," said Vicky.

Summer grinned. "Voodoo probably does have a flock of andies he's using," he said. "That's what Ezra Zilber was trying to tell me. He wanted me to know that the Tin Mahatma wasn't the only android around."

"Blamsakes, that was sure some nap." Finity appeared in the doorway, hair tangled and eyes still a bit unfocused.

"You're supposed to be snoozing until way into tomorrow." Palma scooted over to her, slipped an arm around her waist.

"Shux, stunguns never knock me out for as long as they do most folks," she said, laughing. "I've got a real strong constitution."

"I don't," said Vicky, "believe we've met."

"Vicky, Finity. Finity, Vicky." Summer was glancing around the lab. "Some stunguns over in that cabinet yonder, Palma. Let's borrow a few and then work out a plan for getting the hell away from here."

20

With a tacky neowool blanket draped over his shoulders, Palma shuffled out of the cave. He yawned, scratched at his hairless head and glanced around him.

The fog was even thicker and it was rolling across the dark swamp, tangling with the mossy tree branches, turning into huge looming shapes. Hundreds of insects were chirping, nightbirds cawed and shrieked.

Palma yawned again.

"Here now." A robed green man materialized from out the swirling fog, his kilgun pointed at the photographer. "You're not supposed to be roaming around, my lad."

"Let me see if I can phrase this as politely as poss—"

"No conversation. March right back inside your—"

"I'm out here hunting for the facilities."

"The what?"

"The john, the crapper, the—"

"Whyn't you say so? There's one right there inside your blooming cavern."

"No?" Palma was amazed. "How could I ever have overlooked that?"

"You'll find it against the righthand wall. One of those portajakes things, portable little room it is."

"Nope, there's nothing like that."

"Sure, there is."

"Listen, a man who had two heaping bowls of firerat stew a few hours ago is going to be most interested in the location of the biffy right about now," Palma assured him. "I'm telling you I searched high and—"

"Come along, I'll show you the blinking thing."

Palma went in with the guard following. "It's not in here," he persisted.

The green man halted and pointed across the cavern. "There she is yond—"

Zzzzzzzummmmmmmmm!

While the guard's attention was briefly elsewhere, Palma had whizzed his borrowed stungun out and used it.

Swinging off his cot, Summer hurried over. "Four more to go."

They carried the unconscious guard over, dumped him in Summer's cot and covered him with Palma's blanket.

"You be right careful out there," cautioned Finity. "Fact is, I surely believe I ought to tag along to help you fellers with—"

"The fewer of us sneaking around in the swamp," said Summer, "the less chance to screw up."

Vicky reminded, "I'm a crack shot, you know."

"Even so." Summer and Palma moved to the mouth of the cavern. "C'mon, Scoop. This is where you put your act on."

"I'd almost rather have a parasite on my brain than take orders from you two," said the robot. "It truly lacks dignity when—"

"Move," said Palma.

His metallic sigh shook the mechanical man's chest. Muttering, he went clomping out into the misty night.

Quietly, Summer and Palma followed.

"Jack told you not to," said Vicky, who was standing next to Finity just outside the cavern.

"No, he didn't, honey. He was talkin' about us not goin' out an' helpin' them decoy the rest of them guards."

From out of the billowing fog came the sound of Scoop's voice. "Guard, this way quickly. Something terrible's taken place in the cave."

"What's that you—"

Zzzzzzzummmmmmmmm!

Nodding, Finity took a few steps down across the rocky ground. "What I got in mind don't have nothin' at all to do with stunnin' guards."

"I know, but—"

"Hush a minute, hon', and let me concentrate."

"Are you certain, you know, that you're fully recovered?"

"I feel like I just about am," answered Finity. "An' this'll settle the question." Hands on hips, she gazed into the mist.

Her eyes closed, her hands turned to fists.

Nearly a moment later a faint rattling was heard up in the thick fog.

Then, with a clattering woosh, a landtruck fell out of the night to land, bouncing and rattling, on the ground ten yards from them.

Opening her eyes, Finity laughed. "Not near as pretty as the landvan we lost off in that dang hole, but it'll more than get us clear of this ol' swamp."

"That's," said Vicky quietly, "very impressive."

"Ain't it, though," agreed Finity.

"Holy moley!" Palma hopped a pace backward. "I have the distinct impression a truck just flew by."

"Finity probably arranged for our transportation out." Summer straightened up after disarming the last of the fallen green guards.

"Shall we join the ladies then?"

Summer rubbed at his chin. "Not quite yet," he said. "We haven't learned enough."

"We've learned, old buddy, that dozens of foul-tempered green men are snoozing in that camp yonder," said the photographer.

"Scoop!" called Summer.

The cambot was standing a few feet away, his camera lens aimed at a silent hootowl who was perched on a low branch. "Do you have some further demeaning task for me to—"

"Stored in with all your special equipment, do you have a truthdisc?"

"Such devices—I assume you're alluding to the little gadget that allows you to get nothing but honest answers from your hapless victim—are against all the basic laws of robot—"

"Do you have one?"

"As a matter of fact, purely in the interest of thoroughness, I believe I did pack one away with—"

"I'd like to borrow it."

"Listen, pappy, I belong to Vicky and I—"

"Scoop, I don't want to have to take you apart again with a fork and a hairpin, but—"

"Very well. To avoid violence to my cherished person, I'll compromise my code of ethics." Snorting, he tapped his left side. A small door swung open. The robot, unenthusiastically, poked his glittering forefinger into the compartment within. "Let's see now . . . sewing kit . . . metal polish . . . yes, here it is." He extracted a small flat disc of coppery metal, flung it in Summer's direction.

Catching it, he said, "Much obliged."

Scoop shut his side with a slam. "Don't confide in me as to what foul crimes and misd—"

"Go over and look after Vicky and Finity," Summer told him. "We'll be back, in about ten minutes."

"We ought to move out sooner than that." The robot went trotting off into the mist.

Palma rubbed night moisture from his scalp. "What exactly are we up to?"

"Going to do a bit of kidnapping of our own," answered Summer.

21

The encampment, muffled in chill fog, was spread out across a tree-surrounded hollow.

Palma, who was crouched beside the camp guard he'd just stungunned, was squinting through the underbrush at the fifty-odd tentpods. "I'd guess," he said, "that Salesman Sam was residing in that yellow tent over there."

"Since it's twice the size of any of the others," said Summer, "that's pretty likely."

"When you said kidnap, you didn't mean you wanted to haul the shaggy gent off with us?"

"Nope, I just want to get him out of his tent and here in the brush for a private chat."

Nodding, Palma began disrobing the fallen guard. "Shall we do our captive and prisoner routine?"

"An old favorite of mine."

As soon as the photographer was wearing the green man's robe and burnoose, he and Summer started down the mossy incline toward the oversized yellow tent.

". . . have to live with these affirmations," a deep confident voice was intoning within the tent they figured must house the apeman. "So get yourself in the habit of repeating these Villainy Affirmations each and every day: One. Villainy is good. Two. I deserve all I can grab. Three. Looting is just fine for . . ."

Palma eased the tent flap open with the barrel of his stungun. "We've come to the right address," he whispered as he went inside.

Summer followed.

Spread out on a floating airbed, wearing a pair of candystripe pajamas, was Salesman Sam. His eyes were shut, his paws folded over his hairy chest. On the bedside stand sat a tokbox that was playing the self-improvement lecture.

". . . Six. My greed is good for me. Seven. I deserve to conquer . . ."

Sensing something, the sleeping apeman groaned, started to sit up.

Summer lunged and snapped the truthdisc against his temple. It didn't take hold the first try. He had to grab the apeman's thick neck and hold the furry head still. He succeeded the second time.

"Good evening, gentlemen," said Salesman Sam. "To what do I owe this nocturnal intrusion?"

"We'd like you," Summer told him, "to come for a stroll with us."

"That certainly sounds like it'll be a great deal of fun for all concerned." His eyes glazed, Salesman Sam rose from his bed.

Palma took hold of his arm, led him out into the fog. "Lady I was courting on Barafunda once some years back—you may recollect my mentioning the lass with the two lefthanded yonkers—had a husbnad, an exec in the space colony siding trade, who owned no less than sixty-seven pairs of jammies exactly like these bedecking our hirsute—"

"Let's wend our way in silence."

After they'd brought the mind-controlled apeman into the misty woods, Palma sat him down on a fallen log. "She often became quite joyful whenever I donned a pair of the old boys pj's and performed certain—"

"Sam." Summer squatted facing him. "You're going to tell us what we want to know."

"That I am," he agreed. "It'll be a real pleasure to blurt out all I know and betray any and all secrets entrusted to me."

"First off, who's Dr. Voodoo?"

"The top man in his field and, believe you me, a

legend in his own time. If you want the best Zombium deal your money can buy, then you owe it to yourself to trade with Dr. Voodoo."

"I want to know the guy's true identity."

Salesman Sam replied, "That I don't know."

"You've never seen Dr. Voodoo?"

"Never seen him, never talked to him. All my orders are conveyed by messenger. Likewise the regular and dependable payment of my handsome six-figure salary."

"Is he tied in with *Hollywood II?*"

Nodding, the apeman answered, "To the best of my limited knowledge, he is indeed."

"Okay, the *Hollywood II* has landed on Murdstone. Is another shipment of Zombium going to be smuggled out on the spaceship?"

"You bet your life it is."

"How?"

"Once again I have to disappoint you as to details."

"How much do you know about it?"

"Only that tomorrow at midday a large shipment will leave from our plant number 6 in the Great Woodlands," said the truth-telling apeman. "That shipment will be taken to a pickup point in the vicinity of the *Galaxy Jane* location shooting."

"Where's that pickup spot?"

"I haven't that information, gentlemen."

Palma asked him, "What about this number 6 setup? Where exactly is that?"

"In the ruins."

"The same ruins where you were originally going to drag Vicky Nugent?" Summer asked.

"No," said Salesman Sam, shaking his furry head. "This area abounds with ruins and this is a different locale entirely. A delightful and picturesque ruined temple some twenty-six miles due south of us. Once, many centuries ago, this choice setting was occupied by a serpent worshipping cult. Nowadays it's known to local residents as Snake Mama's."

"Finity'll know where that is," said Palma.

Summer said, "Sam, you're going to fall asleep right here in the woods. In fifteen minutes you'll awaken, trot on back to your yellow home, go back to bed and sleep once more. You won't remember any of this."

"That'll be pleasant, since that way I won't know I've betrayed those who've put their trust in me."

"Exactly. Now, drop off to sleep."

The apeman's head tilted forward, his chin thumping his chest. He commenced snoring.

Summer took back the truthdisc. "Off we go to Snake Mama's," he said.

In his dream several dozen green alimony hunters were trundling Summer off to Debtor's Prison in a huge rattling baby carriage that had a defective rear tire.

The rattling grew increasingly harsh and he awakened.

"I didn't mean to spoil your nap," apologized Vicky, who was sitting next to him on the floor of the rear compartment of the rattling landtruck.

He gritted his teeth, yawned, blinked. "Wasn't aware I'd been napping."

"For a couple hours."

"Old codgers need plenty of rest," observed Scoop. The camera robot was seated across the shadowy compartment from them.

"What did I tell you about snide remarks?"

"It's difficult to repress my native wit."

"Well, you sure better make more of an effort or I'm going to have you overhauled soon as we get back to civilization."

Scoop snorted and let his eyes click shut.

Summer said, "Why were you apologizing for waking me?"

"Well, it's sort of dumb," replied Vicky. "What I mean is, I kissed you on the cheek just now. The reason for that, which is kind of dippy, is I've been feeling very grateful to you. For rescuing me from the green men of Gravespawn and all."

"Palma and Finity did as much as I did."

"But they're up in the cab driving this clunk," she said. "And, well, I'm sort of afraid of Palma. That is, you know, if I kissed him in a grateful way he might misunderstand. There's a look he gets in his eyes that—"

"That's mostly because he's a photographer," said Summer, "and sees everything as potential subject matter for his—"

"Applesauce," remarked Scoop without opening his eyes.

"Sometimes, Scoop, you make me feel like the mother of an unruly brat," Vicky said. "Do you have children, Jack?"

"None."

"How long exactly, if you don't mind my asking, were you married?"

"Several long years."

"What sort of person was she?"

"Complex."

"What was her name? No, wait. I looked that up in your NewzNet file before we teamed up." Vicky stared up at the neometal ceiling of the bouncing truck. "Maryella Peterkin Summer. That's sort of a dippy name."

"Which?"

"Peterkin. What I mean is, I'm almost nearly sure that the word 'peterkin' is a euphemism for the . . . um . . . male whatnot on some remote planet or other."

"In an infinite universe almost everything is a euphemism for the male whatnot."

"Yes, I suppose. Maryella isn't all that socko a name either. Did you call her that?"

"As opposed to what?"

"Did you call her, I mean, Mary or Ella or M.E. or Ellie or what?"

"Mostly I called her angelcake."

"This annoys you, doesn't it? My playing investigative reporter with your private life."

"A first-rate reporter could've found out most of what you're asking me without ever asking me."

"Well, as a matter of fact, I did," she admitted. "But I'm looking for those little details that only a prime source can give you, you know."

"The marriage didn't work," he said. "I'd thought it would."

"Okay, I'll cease," she said. "Here's a question on an entirely different topic. Would it unsettle you too much if I kissed you? To express my gratitude only, while you're wide awake?"

"Not at all." He put an arm around her, turned her to him and kissed her.

"Mush," muttered Scoop.

22

"Impressive." Palma lowered his binoculars and swatted again at the flock of tiny red gnats that was circling his bald head. "There's a religion that knew what was important in life."

They were hidden on a wooded hillside above the ruined temple that served Dr. Voodoo as his number 6 Zombium processing plant. The temple was shaped like a sawed-off pyramind. Standing, arms raised high, on a pedestal before the main entrance was a gigantic stone woman. She had snakes—dozens of them—for hair and three pairs of breasts. The breast motif was repeated on the walls of the temple itself and in the weedy, overgrown tile courtyard.

"Imagine a set of kazebos that large," mused Palma, aiming one of his cameras at the scene. "Take you an afternoon to fully explore just one. You'd have to use mountain-climbing gear to—"

"Honest to Pete, Palma," said Finity, "I never seen anybody so wrapped up in his hobby."

Summer was watching the temple through an electro-spyglass. "It's getting close to midday," he said. "What are you picking up, Scoop?"

The cambot had his lens and his built-in sound rod aimed at the vine-covered temple. "I estimate there are something like ten hooligans at work inside the temple."

"Plus six more patroling the rim as guards," said Vicky. "Too many for us to tangle with, don't you think, Jack?"

"I don't want battles just yet," he said. "We just follow the shipment when it leaves here and see how, and with whom, it makes its way aboard the *Hollywood II*."

"That's going to be," put in the robot, "trickier than expected, pappy."

"How so?"

"I'm monitoring fragments of their conversation. One of the lunkheads just mentioned that 'dah skycar is gonna be here any minute.' "

"Skycar?" Summer let the hand that was holding the spyglass drop to his side. "This is a restricted area. They can't fly over the—"

"Could it be," suggested the robot, "that dope smugglers are not above breaking other laws?"

"What Jack's getting at is that they can't fly far," said Palma, "without risking being spotted by a patrol."

"Blamsakes, there it is now." Finity pointed skyward.

A dull green skycar, chuffing and backfiring, was dropping down out of the hazy midday.

A catman in a two-piece worksuit came rushing from out the temple. He scooted up the steep stone steps to the platform atop it. Two more catmen, each hefting a heavy black suitcase, followed him at a slower pace.

"That's got to be the Zombium," said Vicky.

Summer reached into a pocket. "Finity," he asked, "can you teleport something from here into one of those suitcases?"

"I surely can."

He passed her a tiny tracking bug. "If we can plant this with the Zombium, then we can trail the shipment even if they do fly off."

After examining the little disc of dark metal for a few seconds, she said, "Okay, there she goes." It quivered and was gone from her palm.

Down on the stone platform one of the catmen gave a small hop and then frowned down at the suitcase in his paw.

The skycar was landing on the platform, sputtering and trailing sooty smoke.

"Let's get back to our truck," said Summer.

"Soon as I take a few more shots of Snake Mama," said Palma.

Summer, the small tracking screen held in his hand, was sharing the cab of their borrowed landtruck with Finity. "They just changed their course and are flying in a northwesterly direction."

"Danged if I don't think I can guess where they're

headin'." She was driving with both hands on the wheel.

The roadway was narrow, full of thick shadows thrown by the branches of the twisted trees. Faintly glowing monkeys were following their progress, swinging through the branches and vines on a parallel course.

"Where?" asked Summer.

"We'll be hittin' another crossroads 'bout three miles ahead," she answered. "If you take it to the right you end up, after some twenty bumpy miles, at a town name of East Hellspore."

"Sounds like a lively place."

"Ain't near as bad as West Hellspore, which is way the heck on the other side of the Fiery Desert," Finity told him. "Plenty rough enough, though. Wide-open town where slavers, smugglers, assassins and other assorted scum gather. Along with a few venturesome tourists."

"Just the sort of spot they might be delivering the load of Zombium to." Summer was watching the tracking screen again.

"Them fellers in that skycar won't want to fly too far, since they might be spotted. More 'an like they'll drop her down in Hellspore," she said. "Then either continue on by land or turn the stuff over to someone else."

"Maybe turn it over to somebody from the *Hollywood II* crew."

"Sounds more than . . . Oh, shux." She braked, stuck her head out the window. "G'wan, you dimwit critter, scoot!"

A fat female unicorn was munching flowers that grew at the road edge and blocking their way.

Impatient, Finity hit the shockwave horn button.

When the wave hit the unicorn, she stiffened, stared at the truck, swallowed a mouthful of crimson flowers and waddled off into the shadows.

Finity started their truck rolling again. "Somethin' else I been meanin' to ask you."

"Go ahead."

"Are you havin' a romance with that skinny little Vicky girl?"

"Nope."

"Sure looks to me like she's gone plumb goofy over you. Way she makes grout's eyes at you an' . . . Woops, here's our crossroads. They still headin' for Hellspore?"

"Seem to be."

She swung the truck onto the righthand road.

A flock of black and white peacocks went scattering out of their way.

"I wouldn't exact say she's too young for you or nothin'," resumed Finity. "But, shuxamighty, you've been hooroarin' 'round the planets for near to twenty years, Jack, an' you ought to take up with a woman who's as experienced as you."

"Women who've been around as much as I have tend to be somewhat battered and weatherbeaten."

"Not all of 'em," she assured him.

23

"Behave yourself, Scoop," warned Vicky, "or I'll have you stand out in the hallway."

"That'd leave you alone in this pesthole with pappy here."

"This isn't a pesthole," Summer informed him from the shuttered window. "We happen to have checked into the Imperial Suite."

"The Imperial Suite, need I point out, of a joint that calls itself the Boot In The Arse Inn and whose sign depicts a hobnailed boot in the act of kicking—"

"You've got to quit being so snappish." The young woman joined Summer at the window of their room. "Still there?"

Down in the courtyard of the inn the dull green skycar was parked near the peeling stucco wall. A shaggy catman who'd accompanied the suitcases from the ruined temple was sitting on a wine barrel. The two suitcases of Zombium were still inside the car.

"Yep. Our man keeps listening to his tokwatch."

"Waiting for somebody," concluded Vicky. "Do you think it was safe to let Palma and Finity follow the pilot?"

"Anything Palma can't handle, she can."

"But this is an awfully wild town." She nodded at the view of the twilight street they got through the neowood shutter. "I mean, just look down there at the sort of establishments that share the block with this inn."

The buildings were of stone and peach-colored stucco, capped with lopsided towers and minarets and slanting red tile roofs. Immediately across the street was the Thieves' Market—*Going Out Of Business Sale! Our Loss Is Your Gain! Choice Loot & Plunder At Low, Low Prices!*—and next door to that, with a candy-stripe awning over its carved neowood door, was the local branch of the Thugs & Stranglers Guild. A sidewalk cafe called Ma Guttermouth's was doing a crowded, thriving business farther along the block.

"He's consulting his watch again," noticed Vicky. "Could be his contact is . . . What's that funny sound?"

A wailing, wooshing noise had started up. It grew swiftly nearer.

"Sand storm," said Summer.

Wind and grit came roaring along the street. Three of the round tables in front of Ma Guttermouth's took to the air, shedding their checkered tablecloths, and a fourth went cartwheeling along the flagstone paving. Patrons became airborne as well and burnooses billowed, cloaks flapped, turbans unfurled, derbies left heads. A bolt of contraband neosilk flew by, its yellow and scarlet yards unfurling and snapping. Roof tiles were in flight, too, dozens of them flickering by, clacking and crackling.

Everything turned a greasy dark brown outside, killing the view. The shutters on their room window were suddenly snatched by the wind and went spinning away into the billowing sand.

Summer swung an arm around Vicky's waist, pulled her back from the glaz window just before it exploded inward from the blow of wind-tossed tiles. He tugged her farther into the room, clear of the jagged shower of scattering fragments.

She took hold of him, shivering. "Thanks."

The wail of the sandstorm died all at once. There was an instant of absolute silence. Then noise began filling up the dusky street—shouting, screaming, running.

Letting go of the young woman, Summer ventured back to the window for a look down at the courtyard. "Skycar's still there," he said. "But our catman's gone."

When the sand storm came pushing and howling into

the quirky lane on the north edge of Hellspore, Palma and Finity had been walking unobtrusively along about half a block to the rear of the skycar pilot, a lean lizard-man in a three-piece cazsuit.

Palma was actively pretending to be a tourist. "Just look at that will you, mother? The Modern Noise Quartet is playing an exclusive engagement right here at Bop City," he exclaimed enthusiastically. "And just look who's on first garbage can."

"Honest to Bess," Finity told him in a whisper, "you don't sound no more like a rube tourist 'an I do, Palma honey."

"Sure, I do, Fin. My gift for mimicry is . . . yoiks!" He caught her by the hand and yanked her down into the entry alcove of the nightclub.

"Shuxamighty, what . . . Oh, it's a dang sand storm comin' right at us."

They elbowed the padded door open, went stumbling into the dimlit foyer.

"You folks are in luck," the tuxedoed toad manager told them. "I can seat you at a ringside table near the anvil player if—"

"Actually," explained Palma, "we just came in to get out of the storm."

"C'mon, don't try any of those tried and true deadbeat tricks on . . . Well, I stand corrected."

The sand-laden wind had ripped the door clean off Bop City and carried it on down the lane. Grit came scurrying across the foyer, hot wind blew nineteen hats from the shelves of the checkstand and filched the curly platinum wig from the hatcheck girl's pretty head.

"Ah, a fellow baldy." Palma and Finity backed farther into the place.

"What a town, what a town," grumbled the manager. "That's the fourth damn door I've lost this year already. Two the damn sand storms took, one the cops shot up and . . . Mabel, I forget. How'd we lose the other door?"

The hairless young woman popped a checkered cap atop her head before replying, "I think it was that plague of locust, Bosco."

"Naw, they only ate the neon sign."

"You're right." She snapped her fingers. "Oh, oh, I remember. When the circus came through town and the Human Canonball tried to commit suicide by—"

"You're absolutely right, Mabel, that's it."

The sudden storm suddenly died.

Palma smiled at their host, gave a lazy salute to the hairless girl, and escorted Finity over the scattered derbies, toppers, and knit caps to the gritty sidewalk outside.

"We for certain lost that ol' skycar pilot now," Finity said, glancing unhappily up and down the lane.

"Pretty much sure I spotted him turning to the left up at the corner just before the sand hit." Palma started off up the lane. "If he took cover, he ought to be coming out into the open right about now."

"If he didn't get a chance to hide, maybe he got carried off over the rooftops." She caught up with the photographer. "That was a mighty fierce wind."

The lefthand lane was wider and led downhill, passing by three saloons, a brainstim parlor and a mummydust den before it reached a large open-air market place.

"That's him up ahead," said Palma, "heading for the bazaar."

Down at the edge of the tiled market area a huge catman in a candy-stripe robe and turban was brushing sand out of his fur. That task completed, he lifted a bullhorn to his mouth. "Business as usual, folks," his burred voice came booming. "Storms don't stop us from staging our biweekly Slave Bazaar and Baseball Card Show."

"That's an odd mix," mentioned Palma as they passed the catman.

He lowered his bullhorn. "I'll be honest with you, Mac, the competition in the slave trade is something horrendous these days," he confided. "We keep trying to beef up things. Two weeks ago we sold chocolate chip cookies along with the ladies and—"

"What say you get to barking, Olan?" called a black man from a platform across the square.

"Right you are, Mr. Freddie. Step right up, folks, for . . ."

Mr. Freddie wore a two-piece lime cazsuit and a holster containing two kilguns with matching ivory handles. Down around the five-foot-high platform he stood on, wide-legged, were four burly catmen in pinstripe cazsuits. Each carried a stunrifle.

"Yes sir, ladies and gents, the auction's about to begin," announced Olan. "The girls'll be sold off first, then the baseball cards."

"Crikey," complained a white-suited cyborg, "I just knew it'd be that way. Wait around, wait around."

Palma had been scanning the line of five young women who were being led out toward the stairs of the auction platform by two more armed catmen. "Good gravy," he said, pulling Finity over against a stucco wall.

"What's wrong? You took a turn for the poorish all of a sudden. Did you swallow some sand or—"

"Notice the dark-haired lady who's second in line."

"Kind of cute, ain't she? In an obvious way."

"It's Taffeta Silverstream of the Barnum Drug Bureau," he said.

"You mean somebody went an' captured her an' is havin' the slavers sell her?"

"Apparently so."

Finity exhaled. "Well sir, I guess we better save her from all these lowlifes, huh?"

"Yep, we'll have to," he said. "Even if it means losing track of our skycar driver."

"He sneaked into that bordello yonder, so maybe you can forget him for a spell."

"Okay," muttered Palma, eying the platform some

twenty yards from them. "We'll concentrate on saving Taffeta."

"You wouldn't want, Palma honey, to just wait around an' try to buy her?"

He shook his head. "That'd be too easy."

24

Summer circled the skycar, casually. The two suitcases of Zombium remained resting inside on the corrugated floor of the rear passenger compartment. The anxious catman, however, wasn't anywhere in the vicinity.

Strolling over to a storage shed at the edge of the inn courtyard, Summer glanced into the half open doorway. No lurking catman.

He put his hands in his trouser pockets and, whistling with his tongue pressed against the back of his teeth, wandered out through the arched gateway to the street.

"Any sign of him?" Vicky was leaning against a palm tree.

"Nope, he either snuck off during the sand storm or got wafted off on the wind."

"Might be, you know, he got restless waiting and went out hunting for his contact."

"Scoop can watch the skycar from up there in our room—especially now that there's no glaz to obscure his view," said Summer. "We'll roam for a spell."

As they started walking uphill, Vicky moved closer to him to avoid stepping on the fallen inn sign. "That's not a very realistic backside, is it?" She observed, linking her arm with his. "This mysterious Dr. Voodoo . . . do you have any notions as to his true identity?"

"A few."

"For instance?" She avoided a cluster of smashed ceramic flower pots the desert wind had discarded at the intersection.

"He or she has to be associated with *Hollywood II.*"

"Then Dr. Voodoo could be, you think, a woman?"

"I don't, nope, but I tossed in that possibility to avoid giving the impression I don't have an open—"

"Say, sport," called a frogman who was clinging to a palm tree trunk high above them, "could you maybe assist me in getting down? The blooming wind tossed me up here."

Summer glanced around, noticed a candy-stripe mattress that had been deposited on top of an abandoned eel pie vending wagon. He hefted the mattress over, dropped it at the base of the tree. "Slide on down."

"My problem is, sport, I suffer from extreme vertigo and—"

"No time for therapy." He and Vicky continued along the early evening street.

Vicky said, "You have some . . . Darn, look who just now got tossed out on his ear. Well, actually birdmen don't have ears as we know them."

"Bunch of bubbleheads, you don't even know iambic pentameter from your elbow . . . But wait a minute, kiddo. Why was I in that dive in the first place . . . debating rhyme scemes with three vacationing lesbian dockwallopers? Didn't I . . . Didn't I have some reason for . . . What's the meaning of life anyhow?" Harlan Grzyb, the parrot-headed birdman, had just now been flung through the swinging bamboo doors of the Poetaster Saloon.

Vicky hurried over to him. "Good evening, Mr. Grzyb," she said, extending a hand. "How do you come to be flat on your rump in front of this particular low Hellspore dive?"

He gazed up at her with blurred eyes. "That's a hell of a good question, sis," he answered. "I keep . . . the feeling I have . . . some important rendezvous is being missed." He considered her hand for several seconds before grasping it with his feathery fingers and allowing her to pull him upright.

He remained that way for less than a minute and then lurched against her.

Vicky caught the small feathered screenwriter under his arms, pushed him to a standing position yet again. "That's a nasty bump you have on your head, Mr. Grzyb. Your skull is all dented and . . . dented?"

Reaching out, Summer thumped the birdman's skull.

Ping! Bonk!

"Jack? What's this mean? Where the feathers got rubbed off there's a part of an aluminum skull showing through."

". . . important errand to do . . . that's why I'm in town . . . but brix on the noggin' slowed me down . . ." He brought a hand up to his beak.

"Exactly what happened?" Vicky asked him.

"Sand storm . . . knocked part of a brix wall over . . . conked me on the skonce . . . joggled the keen Grzyb mind all flooey . . ."

"Actually," said Summer quietly, "you aren't Grzyb at all. You're nothing more than an android sim."

"Say, that would explain why I have a metal skull . . ."

Vicky said, "Another one of Dr. Voodoo's androids?"

"Sent, probably, to pick up the Zombium."

"Bingo!" The Grzyb simulacrum chuckled. "Pick up the Zombium . . . put it in my posh landcar . . . tool off to . . . someplace or other, sweetie . . ."

Summer told the android, "We can help you collect your thoughts."

"Haven't we met?" The android studied him. "Are you with the Senior Citizen Grzyb Fan Club?"

"No, more's the pity. I let my dues lapse." Summer put an arm around the android's shoulders. "Just step into that alley over there. We'll have you in tip-top shape in no time."

"And then I'll remember clearly and know everything I'm supposed to be doing?"

"You will," Summer assured him, "and so will we."

Making an impressive series of self-important snorts and murmurs, Palma pushed through the smattering of bidders, gumcard buffs and curious tourists who stood in the bazaar square. Night was coming on and floating yellow globes had winked on overhead. The orange lamps affixed to the high stone wall that ran along one side of the square were also glowing now. Palma's perspiring head and dangling cameras reflected the light as he hurried up to the lineup of slave women about to be sold off.

He winked carefully at the dark-haired Taffeta, who was wearing a stained and tattered two-piece khaki cazsuit. "Fear not," he told her out of the side of his mouth.

"Get your toke back with the other yokels, skinhead," advised the larger of the two escorting catmen.

Ignoring him, Palma brought up one of his cameras, squinted through the viewfinder at Taffeta. "Perfect, absolutely yummy perfect," he said with a sigh that caused his entire body to quiver.

"Hey, cueball." Mr. Freddie was squatting on the edge of the auction platform, scowling at Palma. "What the huff you doing?"

"Absolutely yummy wonderful." Palma paid the angry black man no mind as he started clicking off shots of the manacled Barnum Drug Bureau agent.

"I'm addressing you." Mr. Freddie swung out to thump him on the shoulder.

Palma's sigh was an annoyed one this time. "Don't you ever, ever do that again," he told the slaver. "Not while I'm photographing anything." He glanced casually to his right and saw that Finity was now atop the fifteen-foot-high wall.

"Listen, I don't want no swishy egghead coming in here and taking pictures of my—"

"Do you have any, I mean absolutely any, idea of who I am?" Palma slid a powerful flashgun from beneath his tunic.

"I know you going to be diddly spit in about two—"

"I am none other than Manley Dumpling-Smith of *Vainglory*," Palma explained impatiently while he placed the flashgun on the platform edge. "Even you fellows must've heard of the most distinguished fashion photographer in the universe."

"You can't take no pictures of my merchandise," boomed Mr. Freddie. Growling, he kicked the flashgun off the auction block.

Palma closed his eyes and signaled Finity.

An enormous blinding flash of light exploded from the flashgun.

Palma opened his eyes to see the black slaver's gunbelt slide down to his ankles, tighten and cause him to teeter. Mr. Freddie came tumbling down and hit the ground with an impressive thump.

At that same moment the weapons of the half dozen guards leaped free of their hands to go spinning up and away into the night.

They saw none of this, being still blinded and concentrating on rubbing their eyes, yowling and hopping around.

"The lass is a wonder," said Palma, taking another look at Finity atop the wall.

The four slave girls and Taffeta left the ground, one by one. They floated over the bazaar and the startled crowd to land near Finity up on the high wall.

"We'll probably never get to the baseball cards now," grumbled the cyborg.

"We don't want them all," Palma called toward Finity as he dodged the blind swing of a catman's furry fist.

Then Palma, cameras swinging and banging, was flying up to join the women.

"Blamsakes, honey, we couldn't rescue just only your ol' ladyfriend an' leave these other poor souls in the clutches of them nasty slavers, now could we?"

He considered that for a second. "Right, we'd lose our standing as humanitarians."

"Palma," said Taffeta, "how in the devil did you track me down and work this?"

"It took cunning, my dear, and much self sacrifice," he informed the dark-haired BDB agent. "The full and heart-warming narrative I'll unfold later. Right now I suggest a swift retreat."

"Before them slavers regain their eyesight an' gather up a fresh mess of weapons." Finity led them along the wall and over to the flat roof of an adjoining mosque.

25

Scoop was sitting in a neowicker rocker, watching unobtrusively the courtyard below. "The catman got back here fifteen minutes ago," he said with a quick glance over his metal shoulder. "What sort of lewd hanky-panky delayed you two?"

"It's back to the shop for you," Vicky told him. "Soon as we get home."

"We want footage of what's going to happen below," Summer told the camera robot as he shut the door.

"Why waste vidfilm on an oaf resting his toke on a barrel?"

Crossing the unlit room, Summer said, "Here comes the Grzyb sim. Film this transaction, Scoop."

Groaning, the robot left the rocker. "Isn't one offensive pint-sized bird writer enough? Why construct a replica?"

"It helps with the smuggling."

The cambot was whirring now, capturing the scene that was unfolding down in the dimlit courtyard. "This isn't the stuff of drama," he commented. "Grzyb shakes hands with catman. Catman opens skycar. They drag out the two suitcases full of Zombium. Birdman grabs one with each hand. Goes tottering out of courtyard and off camera. Even my expert cinematography isn't going to pep up this—"

"Quit your belittling," advised Vicky.

The robot ceased filming. "Oughtn't we to be trailing the feathery shrimp?"

"We know where he's going." Summer opened the door. "Let's get back to the truck and then see about rounding up Finity and Palma."

"How, if I may ask, do you know where the Zombium's going next?"

"That information," said Vicky, following Summer out of the room, "was all stored in the andy's head, along with a heck of a lot of other interesting stuff."

"There are times," said Scoop, "when I don't feel at all like an equal partner in this venture."

"And so we bid a fond farewell to Hellspore," said Palma as their landtruck rattled through the ragtag outskirts of town.

"Now explain to me in greater detail who all those ladies we have stuffed in the back compartment are." Summer was driving and he and the photographer were the only occupants of the cab.

"Speaking of which, Taffeta Silverstream of the Barnum Drug Bureau is ticked that you wouldn't allow her to ride up here with us."

"So is Vicky," he said. "I want to go over this whole business with you before we share anything with the law. About your entourage?"

Palma fished a crumpled memo slip out of a trouser pocket. "I gathered this info on the run, whilst fleeing crazed slavers through the fetid lanes and byways of Hellspore," he explained. "In addition to Taffy, we have with us Olga Haringo . . . she's the one with the startled chonkers . . . by that I mean they give you the impression they're standing up poised for flight. Next there's Princess Sekerup. Her jazzbos are petite, as befits a princess, and the left one appears to be . . . and keep in mind I gathered this data on the run . . . slightly out of alignment or—"

"Simply tell me how you acquired them."

"Fin and I boldly rescued the damsels from a slave bazaar. I really only wanted to save Taffeta, but Finity convinced me that we were obliged to go for the whole and entire—"

"About dawn we ought to hit a relatively safe settlement on the edge of the desert. They can be let off there and arrange for transportation."

"Could I impose on you to snap a few shots of my escorting the ladies to freedom?" He tapped at one of his cameras. "There's a possibility I can peddle a picture feature to *Musclebound Men's Adventures* or some similar literary organ."

"How'd Taffeta end up on the auction block?"

The last lights of Hellspore were gone and the truck rolled through dark open fields.

"She dropped into town to check on a rumor that a big shipment of Zombium was coming through," answered Palma. "While frequenting a low dive—come to think of it, there are no other kind of dives in Hellspore—she was doped. Came the dawn she was in the slavers' showroom awaiting the latest auction. Only a kind fate and my expert heroics saved the lass from—"

"Her tip about the Zombium was right."

"Sure, that was the two bagsful we've been tailing hither and yon," said Palma. "Where, by the way, has that stuff gotten to?"

"It's en route to Fort Blumenkohl in the Fiery Desert. Being driven there in Harlan Grzyb's neon-trimmed sportscar."

"By Grzyb?"

"Nope, by an android replica."

"More of Dr. Voodoo's handiwork."

Summer guided the landtruck around a deep rut in the dusty roadway. "Voodoo's got six of them ready to be loaded with Zombium," he said. "The batch includes the Flo Haypenny andy we last saw at the caverns."

"He's going to have to improve her yonkers before he can really fool anybody," said Palma. "And what of the real Flo, Grzyb, et al?"

"Fort Blumenkohl is the actual Royal Mounted Stungunners base that figured in the battle being recreated in *Galaxy Jane*. Green men versus the military," said Summer. "Fort itself has been shut down for near fifty years or so. The *Hollywood II* folks sent out a crew some months ago to spruce it up so it could be used in the movie. They built, unbeknownst to many, a few new underground rooms beneath the place. That's where the Zombium's going and where Flo and the others are being held."

"Okay, Dr. Voodoo loads his imitations up with Zombium, then ships them out on the *Hollywood II* soon as shooting on *Galaxy Jane* is finished." Palma stroked his fuzzy moustache. "What about the actual Flo Haypenny all that time?"

"After the Zombium's safely on Barnum, the *Hollywood II* will come back out here to Murdstone," explained Summer. "The real people are switched with the androids, after having been brainwiped and given some false memories. Nobody's the wiser."

"And Dr. Voodoo is several million trubux richer." Palma nodded. "Did you deduce all this, old buddy?"

"Quite a bit I got from the Grzyb android," he admitted. "He got bopped with brix during that sand storm and it futzed his inner workings some. We ran into him and I repaired him. While I was tinkering I got him to tell what he knew."

"Too bad he wasn't aware of the true identity of Voodoo."

"He knew that."

Palma sat up. "So who?"

"Think about it," suggested Summer.

"Naw, I've been running mini-marathons with escaped slave girls. My thinking equipment isn't up to the task."

"Dr. Voodoo has to be associated with the *Hollywood II*," said Summer. "Has to be somebody fairly high up so he can be aware of the ship's comings and goings in advance and, when he has to, arranging a side trip or a return to Murdstone."

"That does narrow the field of suspects some," said

Palma. "Although Dr. V. could just be a guy who works in the galley and has a tricky way of tapping the ships' computer."

"When he stopped Flo Haypenny from talking to me, he didn't do her any harm," said Summer. "Same with Zilber. And Zilber was finished with his work on *Haunted Mansions* before he was given that overdose of Zombium."

"So it's somebody who has an interest in the financial well-being of the *Hollywood II* productions." Palma tugged at one end of his moustache and gazed out at the darkness. "He didn't want to permanently foul up the stars or staff of the movies in production."

"Yep, and he didn't want to kill any NewzNet reporters because that would mean bad publicity for *Hollywood II*."

"I'm getting a hunch," said the photographer. "When Zilber tried to tell you something, he muttered something like, 'The Tin Mahatma isn't the only one.' He meant he'd found out about the android sim business . . . but maybe he also meant that the lads who built the Tin Mahatma were making the facsimiles, too."

"He did," said Summer, grinning. "What we've been going up against on this has been some extra special special effects."

"Provided by none other than the Swain Brothers."

"Slim and Slam Swain are Dr. Voodoo."

"We better tell Taffeta."

"After we get to the fort," said Summer, "and spring Flo and the rest."

26

Palma moved enthusiastically along the sandstone steps of the skybus depot. "Bon voyage, Princess Sekerup," he said cordially, bestowing a hug on the handsome platinum-haired young woman.

"I am . . . how you say in your own tongue, Mr. Palma . . . most grateful to you."

"No words called for, princess." He kissed her on one cheek and then the other.

The night was ending, the thin light of dawn was moving into the streets of Hotspot Corners. The low brix and stucco buildings were turning a pale gold, fragile mist was rising from the stone fountain in the center of the small dusty plaza.

"I'm damn fond of Palma," remarked Taffeta Silverstream, "but there are times when I wish he was less outgoing." She was standing near the parked land-truck, watching the photographer bid the four rescued young women farewell.

Summer, using one of Palma's cameras, was taking pictures of the event. "For Palma, this is rather subdued behavior."

"So long, Olga." Palma hopped to a higher step to throw his arms around an ample redhead.

"I'll miss you, sugar, even though I really didn't get to know you too good."

"A few minutes with me is like a year, at least, with an ordinary lad." He kissed her on the lips.

Taffeta edged closer to Summer. "You know a hell of a lot more about that Zombium shipment than you've told me."

"True," he agreed.

"Listen, I know all about how you operate. Keeping back information, trying to outfox the law, using every sort of sneaky dodge to—"

"You're coming with us to the fort," he said, turning to face the BDB agent. "Once we take care of a few things there, I'll tell you everything . . . well, nearly everything I know about Dr. Voodoo and his operations."

"Damn it, Summer, that could be too late. If you make me futz up the—"

"Nevertheless, that's how we—"

"I can really screw up your life," she warned. "Make things damn rough for—"

"Nope, nobody can screw up my life but me." He grinned as he slipped the camera back into its case. "And if you keep playing tough cop with me, I'll toss you on the next skybus out of here."

She made an angry noise, spun on her booted heel and went walking away from him.

Vicky came over to him now. "Has she been browbeating you, Jack?"

"We were merely chatting about Palma's winning ways."

The young woman shuddered briefly. "I sort of like him, but I don't think I'd want him kissing me in the ear the way he's doing to that green-haired girl," she said. "Well, anyway. I've noticed a sort of nice-looking place where we might have breakfast. See it over on the corner there? Granny Grail's Cozy Cafe. Nice clean white lace curtains at the windows, bright Venusian tulips in the flower boxes. It ought to—"

The door of Granny Grail's came slamming open. A husky groutherder came sailing out headfirst, clutching most of a lace-trimmed tablecloth. Clearing the three spotless realwood front steps, he landed elbows first in the dust of the early morning road. A hairy paw appeared in the doorway to fling a flower-trimmed china plate of tiny griddle cakes and blue parsley out after the ejected customer.

"Around here, stranger, we don't take kindly to complaints about our garnish," growled the voice that went with the hairy arm.

"Looks like," said Summer, "our kind of place."

The wooden gates of the sprawling stone fort were open wide and Finity drove the truck right on into the flagstone courtyard and out of the hot yellow glare of the desert. "Blamsakes, I surely hope they got this here place air-conditioned," she said, edging the dusty vehicle around a mob of actors dressed in the handsome blue and gold uniforms of Royal Mounted Stungunners of nearly a century earlier.

An assistant director, a blond catman in a one-piece purple smocksuit, came running over toward them as Finity parked near a large corral filled with horses and grouts. "You can't park there—it spoils the illusion," he shouted. "Destroys the sense of the past."

Summer dropped free of the truck on his side. "We're with the press," he explained, helping Vicky disembark.

"Press or not, you are simply not authentic Galaxy Jane period." He made a shooing motion with both furry blond hands. "Move it over there by those other newsvans, miss."

"It's been making some mighty funny whangin' and thumpin' noises the past few miles," Finity told the assistant director. "I surely hope I can get it to—"

"Try, try," he urged. "Mr. Chiizu is going to start shooting a scene, just as soon as Mr. Yoe gets in the mood."

Shrugging, Finity started the landtruck up and drove it to the acceptable location.

Vicky wiped at her perspiring forehead with a plyochief. "Could Palma and Taffeta Silverstream really have been doing what it sounded like they were doing in the back of our truck?"

Summer stretched, getting rid of a few travel kinks. On the second stretch his left elbow produced a creaking sound. "More than likely."

"But Scoop was riding back there with them," she reminded. "Wouldn't he put a sort of damper on—"

"He can be circumvented."

Over at the center of the high-walled fort's broad courtyard, Bunker King, Jr. suddenly yelped and fell back from a group of writers, associate directors, and associate producers.

The Harlan Grzyb android leaped onto him, feathers quivering, and commenced throwing punches at his face and chest. "Of course the dialogue's banal, thimble-wit," he said between jabs. "Your great grandfather was a banal man, so naturally—"

"He was no such thing. If you'd studied the journals, you'd know . . ."

"The imitation Grzyb is here," observed Summer. "That means the Zombium's been delivered to the hideaway under this place."

Vicky watched the crew separate the writer and the consultant.

"There's a strain of violence in the real Grzyb, too," he said. "It shows in his prose, most especially in *The Beast That Shouted Birdseed at the—*"

"Show business," exclaimed Palma as he came trotting up to them. "Buoys you up, the glamor of it all. Not to mention the frequent brawls."

"What happened to your moustache?" asked Vicky.

The photographer slapped a hand to his upper lip. "It's still there."

"But awfully droopy."

"Humidity takes the curl out of it."

She eyed him from top to toe. "Did you do anything nasty to Scoop en route?"

"Not nasty, no." He smiled, spreading his hands wide. "The poor fellow was complaining of the heat and stuffiness back there, so I obligingly turned him off for the duration of our steamy journey across the blazing sands of—"

"You twerp!" Scoop arrived in their midst. "Rendering me immobile while you canoodle with that lady of the law and—"

"Don't go broadcasting Taffeta's profession in these—"

"Where is she anyway?" asked Vicky.

"Freshening up," answered Palma, glancing around the courtyard. "The false Harlan Grzyb arrived safely I note."

Summer said, "You and Vicky stay out here and give one and all the impression you're fascinated with this aspect of the *Galaxy Jane* shooting. Finity and I and Scoop'll crash the underground—"

"That's not exactly fair, Jack," protested Vicky. "I'm a crack shot, as I have to keep reminding—"

"You're also someone a lot of the guys hereabouts will notice," he told her. "That's what a diversion is all—"

"I'm flattered, but—"

"Dangsakes," said Finity. "Let's quit squabblin' an' get movin'."

"Soon as Palma and Vicky get over to where our fake Grzyb is carrying on," said Summer, "we'll sneak below, Finity."

She looked around. "Them brix buildings over yonder must be the ones the andy told you about, don't you think, Jack, honey?"

"Yep, that's where we'll head. C'mon, Scoop."

"I suppose tagging along with you is better than witnessing any further lewd acts," murmured the robot.

27

Summer led the way into the store room. "This is exactly the sort of background stuff we want, gang," he said loudly, gesturing at the assorted fake palm trees, mock weapons and other props that filled the windowless stone-walled room. "Roll 'em, Scoop."

"A bit thick," muttered the camera robot, pretending to whir.

"I swear you got a worse disposition than my Cousin Lunk," said Finity.

"Folks, I'm afraid this is off limits. I'll have to request that you drag your respective keasters on out." A lizardman carrying a stunrifle stepped out from behind a prop palm tree.

"Give me a nice close-up of this guy," requested Summer.

"Coming right up, boss." The robot moved up close to the guard. "I'll use soft focus to remove all these warts, wrinkles, scales—"

"Cease your inventory right there, pal," ordered the guard. "And do a scramola."

Summer said, "It's okay, we're with NewzNet. Tell us how it feels to be part of an exciting space pirate epic like *Galaxy Jane.*"

"I'm telling you to haul your butts out. Nobody's allowed in this part of the . . . ooops!"

His stunrifle left him. He himself was turned upside down and lifted to the stone ceiling high above them.

Summer watched the dangling lizardman for a bit. "The electrakey to the trap door."

"You're talking to a stranger. I've got no idea what . . . Ooof!"

Finity let the guard drop half way toward the stone floor before stopping him and lifting him back to the ceiling.

"The key," Summer urged.

"Damned if I enjoy these ethical decisions," said the guard. "Torn between self-interest and . . . hey!"

The jacket of his two-piece yellow cazsuit became agitated, undulating and turning its pockets out. A silver key floated free of a pocket, came drifting gently down to land in Finity's upheld hand. "You don't have to fret none now. You can just tell 'em we stole it from off you." She passed the key to Summer.

"Door's supposed to be under those crates over there. Scoop, help me move them."

The cambot said, "Far as I know the vidmovie industry is highly unionized. To have a camera do the work of—"

"Proceed."

"Shuxamighty. I'll do it."

Six heavy neowood cases slid ten feet to the left. In the stone floor below where they'd been sitting was a plaz panel the size of a room door.

Crouching, Summer inserted the electrakey in the sechole.

In less than ten seconds the sound of a hooting alarm was heard down below.

"Obviously," said Summer, "the Grzyb andy didn't tell us everything."

"My turn to grandstand," said Scoop as the muffled alarm ceased down below. He pointed his left ring finger at the plaz panel. "Stand aside, pappy."

Summer complied.

Zzzzzzzzaaaannnkkkkkk!

The floor panel keened, quivered and then turned to purplish soot. The only thing now stopping them from going down the slanting ramp to the secret rooms below was the bulky apeman standing in midramp with a kilgun in each fuzzy fist.

Zzzzzzzummmmmmm!

Summer was faster with his stungun than the apeman was with either of his kilguns.

Before the apeman had hit the pebbled surface of the ramp Summer was starting down it.

"Be real careful, Jack honey." Finity hurried after him.

Scoop brought up the rear, camera whirring.

Finity offered, "I'll fix this next goon."

The toad guard at the ramp bottom executed a somersault, lost possession of his kilrifle and did an impressive headstand.

Zzzzzummmmmmm!

Summer stunned him as they ran by.

The guard stayed upside down and balanced on his turbaned head until Scoop brushed by and caused him to tip over.

They incapacitated four more guards before reaching the room where the two suitcases of Zombium and most of the prisoners were.

"It's about flapping time somebody came to our rescue," said Halran Grzyb as Summer stepped across the stungunned catman guard slumped on the threshold. "Those pinheads are probably desecrating my *Galaxy Jane* script even as we—"

Summer scanned the room. There were several crates of real weapons—stunguns and kilrifles—stacked high against one wall. "Where's Flo?"

Grzyb scratched at the feathers near his beak. "You're not *Hollywood II* staff, are you? Wouldn't you know it. Sure, they send some crummy muckrake to extricate their most valuable—"

"Flo?"

"Big dogman guard took her off to his quarters about an hour ago," answered the feathered screenwriter.

"I'm not even going to imagine what foul and scummy acts he—"

"Where's his room?"

"Two doors down on the right. Now about transportation out of—"

"You don't need to worry about that none," Finity assured him. "They done brought the movie to you."

"What's the pea-brained broad babbling about?"

Summer left the white-walled room, sprinted along the white-walled corridor to the door of the dogman's room.

The door was not quite shut and he could hear what was occurring inside.

". . . and here you are in *Queen of the Lumberjacks* . . . no, wait. This glossy still is from *Sweetheart of the Skymines*. I just absolutely loved you in that, Miss Haypenny. And I'm ever so glad I have this opportunity to show you my scrapbooks and share my feelings. Now, here's the pressbook for *Queen*. To me, you never looked lovelier than you did in that. The way your auburn hair . . ."

Frowning, Summer kicked the door suddenly open wide.

". . . could you just autograph this still where you and Francis X. Yoe, as Pierre of the Woods, are clinching—Good gravy!"

Zzzzzzzzzummmmmmmmm!

Before the dogman could get up off the lucite sofa and out from under the five fat scrapbooks he was sharing with the real Flo Haypenny, the beam of Summer's stungun took him in the chest. He went rigid, then toppled off the sofa and hit the white floor along with the scrapbooks. Loose photos and clippings went skating over the carpeting.

Flo, who was dressed in her Galaxy Jane costume, smiled and stood. "Guess this proves it doesn't pay to be a fan of mine," she said.

28

Francis X. Yoe's gilded spurs jingled, his chest medals tinkled. Pacing in front of the corral, he slapped at his thigh with his riding crop. "I've lost the mood," he complained. "All these unsettling revelations about drug smuggling and chicanery—not to mention there being *two* Harlan Grzybs. *One* is almost more than I—"

"I heard that snide aside, dimbulb," called the true Grzyb from the canvas chair he was lounging in.

Kedju Chiizu, the toadman director, was pacing along with the star. "Frank, listen, we're losing the light," he said. "These delays—all these unmaskings, that lady from the Barnum Drug Bureau making arrests—it's robbed us of time. So what I want you to do right now is the scene where you address your loyal Royal Mounted Stungunners here in the courtyard. You tell all hundred and some of them that you know they're fearful of going up against the Tin Mahatma and his howling hordes of crazed green men. You admit that you're a bit scared yourself, but that your duty to your planet calls for—"

"My great-grandfather wasn't afraid of anything." Bunker King, Jr. came rushing over to them. "Why can't you people ignore this insipid script and present him as he really—"

"How'd you like a punch in the kisser?" asked Grzyb, hopping free of his chair.

"Oh, you already did that."

"Not me, kiddo. You're talking about what that cheap imitation . . ."

Turning his back on the discussion, Summer walked over to where Vicky was sitting beneath a cluster of believable palm trees. "We'll be heading for the location camp, about twenty miles south of here, soon as the BDB agents Taffeta contacted get here to take charge of all of Dr. Voodoo's crowd."

"I don't feel any too zippy," she informed him, slumping further in her canvas chair. "What I mean is, this assignment is pretty near over. After that, you know, we'll go our separate ways, scattering to the far ends of the universe probably."

"We have to go back to Barnum first," he reminded her. "Up in Studio One we have to edit all the vidfilm Scoop's been getting, write our voice over copy."

She gave a mild shrug. "That won't take very long. Then we split up for good and all."

"It's possible we'll work together again sometime."

"Sometime," said Vicky. "Well, it's been pretty obvious to me you'd rather pal around with Palma and that overblown Finity than with me. When you went down into the bowels of this dippy fort, you chose to take Finity and Scoop rather than—"

"I'm used to being in charge of whatever job I'm on. That means—"

"Might I intrude on this powwow?" Palma had come hurrying over to them.

"Something wrong?"

"I suspect there is, old chum. Stroll over to the gateway with me, if you will."

Nodding at Vicky, Summer went along with the photographer. "What is it, something out in the desert?"

"I was taking a few shots of the surrounding countryside. Then I noted a rather sizable cloud of dust forming on the horizon."

They walked through the gateway.

"Horsemen. Couple hundred of 'em," said Summer. "Still a few miles off."

"Take a gander through this." Palma handed him his spyglass.

The fast approaching riders were all green men. "Looks like the Gravespawn gang," Summer observed. "But they could just be extras coming over to—"

"Nope, I already checked on that. Nobody's shooting any scenes with imitation green men here today."

"Making these fellows real green men."

"With real kilrifles."

Lowering the spyglass, Summer said, "When we broke into the secret hideaway a few hours ago, an alarm went off down there."

"It must've gone off over at the location camp, too. In close proximity to the Swain Brothers."

Summer pivoted. "We'd best get ready for an attack," he said.

After he finished saddling the dappled stallion, Summer grabbed up his stunrifle and mounted. "No more time to argue," he said.

Chiizu was standing near the open gate of the corral, anxiously watching his actors lead out mounts. "I'm not exactly suggesting that we don't defend ourselves against this oncoming horde, Mr. Summer," he explained. "But if all, or even a goodly portion, of my Royal Mounted Stungunners suffer real injuries, it'll mean more delays and—"

"By nightfall two of *Hollywood II's* major stockholders'll be in the hoosegow. I wouldn't worry about delays." He left the perplexed director and rode over to the gateway of the fort.

The charging green men were still a good mile off. You could see their guns and swords flashing in the waning light of the day, hear their war cries.

". . . Aiii! Kill! Kill! . . ."

Palma was waiting just outside the fort, riding a powerful grout. A grout is something like a horse, something like a cow, and has six legs. "Finity and Scoop have distributed all the stunrifles you found down below. That gives us about a hundred and twenty armed men."

Behind them extras in the glittering blue and gold uniforms of the RMS were riding out to form into columns.

"Summer," called out Francis X. Yoe from the sandy ground. "I really do think I ought to lead this charge."

"The best I can offer is co-leadership."

The handsome actor toyed with some of his medals. "In that case, I believe I'll remain behind," he said. "However, my best wishes for every success on this courageous venture go with you."

"That's the kind of soul-stirring encouragement we need," Palma told him.

"I feel I owe it to *Hollywood II*," said Yoe, "to see that I survive this attack. I am, after all, a valuable property."

"Exactly." Summer grinned. "Now you'd best scoot back inside and hunker down behind something."

"I appreciate your seeing my point of view." He sped back within.

"Well, I'm sure not going to hide behind anything." Vicky, a stunrifle across her saddle, reined up between Summer and Palma.

"You shouldn't be—"

"Well, I'm going anyway."

He looked at her for a few seconds. "Okay." Shifting in his saddle, he waved at the assembled riders. "Fellas, we have to get this in one take. Let's go!"

29

The immense cloud of gritty dust got there first. Then galloping out of it came the howling green men. They waved swords, kilrifles and stunrods.

"Aii! Aiie! Kill the showbiz infidels!"

"Get back the Zombium!"

"Death to one and all!"

Summer leaned forward in the saddle and fired his stunrifle into the horde of oncoming green men. He saw one, then another of the robed riders stiffen and fall.

"Die, matinee idol!"

A broad-bladed sword came flashing across the twilight at him.

Summer got himself and his mount out of the reach of the blade.

He rode on, dropping two more green riders with his stunrifle. The two masses of mounted men were mingling, tangling. There was yelling, the stomping of hooves, the hum and crackle and clank of weapons all around.

Over on Summer's left Vicky screamed, then came an enormous clattering thump.

Turning, Summer saw her horse go down. Vicky flew free of the saddle and hit the sand.

A green man in a candy-stripe burnoose was riding toward her, swinging a double-edged sword. "Death to all starlets!"

Summer aimed and fired.

Zzzzzummmmmmmmm!

He missed hitting the raider, but did manage to stun his piebald horse. It knelt and fell sideways.

Undaunted, the green man untangled himself, went

charging the fallen Vicky on foot.

Summer leaped from his mount, landing a few yards behind the man. He sprinted, lunged and succeeded in tackling him.

They rolled across the hot sand, punching and fouling each other. The raider struggled to get a good chop at Summer with his sword.

Zzzzuummmmm!

Vicky had shot the green man with the stungun from her thigh holster. "Thanks, Jack."

"Same to you." He ran to her side.

A mounted man was riding right for them, taking aim with a kilgun.

"It's my photographer's eye," said Palma as he stunned his seventh green raider. "Unfailing is what—"

"Blamsakes, Palma! Look out!"

"Eh?" He craned his neck to the left, just in time to spot a sword-wielding raider charging him.

Palma swung his stunrifle around.

"Hold on, honey," said Finity from her milk-white grout.

The photographer found himself being lifted clear out of the saddle. He was a good ten feet above his mount when the sword blade came whooshing through the air space he'd been occupying.

Zzzzzzzummmmmmmmm!

Taking advantage of his new location, Palma fired down on his would-be assassin.

The green man yowled and, robe billowing, tumbled from his mount to the sand.

"Stay up there for a spell," called Finity, galloping to another part of the fracas.

"I feel like a carnival target," he said before he resumed firing.

The green man pulled up on his reins, forgetting all

about killing Summer and Vicky. "Aiee! The ghost of Galaxy Jane!"

Flo Haypenny, long red hair flickering and eyepatch in place, had come riding up out of the dust and shouting. "I'm really tired of the way everybody's been exploiting me." She used her stunrifle.

Zzzzzzummmmmmmmm!

"You okay, Jack?" Flo asked while the green raider was falling off his grout.

"Due to your timely appearance, yes."

"Chiizu didn't want me to tag along," the actress said, "but I'm damned mad at just about everybody and this is a great chance to work it off." She galloped off, firing as she went.

"Darn it," complained a nearby actor in the uniform of the Royal Mounted Stungunners, "Flo can use one of these rifles and I can't seem to. Doesn't work like the prop ones at all."

Summer put an arm around Vicky's waist. "Let's work our way over to the sidelines."

"I feel pretty dippy for letting them kill my poor darn horse."

"That's nothing you have to apologize for." He ran her around a sprawl of stunned raiders, right over a wounded grout and toward an open patch of twilight desert.

"Absolutely first-rate stuff." Scoop was on foot, wading his way through the battle and filming it. "This footage is so good even Summer won't be able to botch it up with his inane commentaries. Movie battle turns real. Daring camera robot captures it all."

Palma was still aloft, some fifteen feet above the sands of the desert. He was using one of his cameras now, clicking off shots of the withdrawal of the green man. They were riding off in full retreat. "Fin," he shouted finally, "if you'd be so kind as to lower me down now."

The blond was helping an injured actor back into the saddle. "Hold on a couple more shakes, Palma, honey."

"No rush," he told her. "I sort of enjoy the view from up here."

30

"Excellent bit of flying, Taffy, my love," commented Palma.

The dark-haired young woman had just landed the Barnum Drug Bureau skyvan at the edge of the *Galaxy Jane* location camp.

"Don't give me any of that romantic guff." The agent unhooked her safety gear. "I saw the way you and that bovine blond were carrying on during the battle this afternoon."

"We were doing naught else but mowing down great numbers of crazed marauders."

Taffeta shoved the cabin door open, made a raspberry sound and dropped out into the warm night. "Floating around above the fighting like some kind of big fat bald-headed bird and calling her Honeypot and Angelcake."

"I've never called a lady Angelcake in my life. You've got me mixed up with Scoop back in the passenger cabin." Cameras jiggling, he jumped out after the angry BDB agent. "Myself, I'm noted for the sweep and imagery of my spoken—"

"And her batting her big slurpy eyes at you. 'Hang on, Palma, dearie.' What tripe."

"Good thing you're not a reporter, the way you misquote the simplest—"

"Just be still now." She drew her stungun from its holster. "I let you and your muckraking cronies come along on this raid against my better—"

"Whoa now, dear Taffy," cut in the photographer. "If Jack and I hadn't yet again used our cunning, you and your thick-witted colleagues there wouldn't have found the stash of Zombium, rounded up most of those involved nor learned the true ID of the notorious Dr. Vood—"

"Eventually I'd have—"

"Oh, so? How were you planning to continue investigating while doing time in the harem of some backwoods toad who—"

"Okay, all right. You did save me from the slave traders," she admitted. "But shut the hell up so we can see if there's any trace of those damn Swain Brothers hereabouts."

The plazhuts glowed faintly in the desert darkness. There were twenty of them circling several landvans.

"The biggest hut," said Summer, "ought to be the one where the Swain boys were residing."

"They're sure to be long gone," commented Vicky.

"No matter, dumpling," said Scoop, his camera whirring. "I'm getting some terrific footage. Night on the rim of the Fiery Desert, the empty house of the drug-ring masterminds giving only mute testimony to—"

The screen door on the biggest hut flapped open. A plump green Swain stepped out, illuminated by a single floating orange globe overhead. "The jig's up," he called out to the approaching party. "We're the first to admit it."

Summer and the others halted about thirty yards from the place. "You ready to surrender?" he asked through cupped hands.

A second Swain appeared on the small porch. "That's just exactly what we intend to do, Summer."

To his rear Taffeta said, "Let me take over, Summer."

Slam Swain called, "We want to talk to Summer before we give ourselves up."

"Yes, that's our wish," confirmed Slim Swain. "We want to give him and that cute little button Vicky an exclusive interview. Then we'll willingly go along quietly with the forces of law and order."

"You bet," added Slam, "cross our hearts."

Vicky nudged the cambot, whispering, "You still have that aura scanner Dad insisted on building into you?"

"Yes, Angel." He casually aimed his thumb at the green pair. "I think I anticipate what you're getting at."

Taffeta came closer to Summer. "I just can't let you go do this," she insisted. "I have to bring in my fellow agents and take these two—"

"Time's wasting," reminded Slam. "Come on up here, Summer, old pal."

"Bring pretty, perky Vicky along, too."

"*Zonk!*" said Scoop's thumb.

Summer said, "Simplest thing is to let me go talk to these—"

"Don't." Vicky took hold of his sleeve.

"Vicky, I can—"

"That's not the Swain Brothers at all."

He looked from them to her. "Androids?"

"Loaded with explosives," added Scoop, tapping his thumb.

Slam said, "They're wise, Slim."

"Let's get even with that bastard Summer anyhow." He started down the steps.

"Scoop!" said Vicky.

Zzzzzzzannnnnnnkkkkkkkkkk!

Two glaring beams of purple light shot forth from the robot's middle fingers. "Hit the deck, folks!"

Catching hold of Vicky, Summer pulled her flat out beside him on the sand.

"Duck, my love." Palma shoved Taffeta over and landed atop her.

The thin lines of blazing light hit the Swains.

"We'll get you yet, Summer!"

"You futzed up our—"

Kaboom!

Kachow! Karoom!

Whump! Whump!

The shock waves slammed at Summer, shoved him and Vicky back along the gritty ground, pushed most of the wind out of him.

The hut and the green andies turned into giant jigsaws and went climbing and rattling up across the darkness.

Then the remains of it all commenced raining down.

"Just as well I didn't interview them," said Summer.

31

The small green editor made a sound that might've been a chuckle. "They want us to do it as a twenty-two-minute NewzDoc Special Report, Jack," he said from behind his lucite desk. "Let me know what you think of these suggested titles for—"

"Nope."

Taliaferro lowered the sheet of pinkish faxpaper he'd just picked up. "Do I hear a negative—"

"The fee you folks paid was for eight minutes of stuff." Summer paced the vufloor, ignoring the view of the planet Barnum down below. "If NewzNet wants three times as much—"

"Three times eight is twenty-four."

"Thanks for supplying those helpful figures. The point is, I want more dough before I edit any vidfilm or write a damn word of—"

"Didn't I mention they've authorized a Special Field Merit Bonus?"

"You didn't, no. How much?"

The NewzNet editor scanned his desk top and located a blue memo. "This is really fairly handsome. Twenty-five thousand trudollars."

"That's not anywhere near handsome, Fred. That's damn close to ungainly and wall-eyed."

"Jack, everybody loves the raw Zombium material and the potential in the whole story. They love you, they love Vicky Nugent. They even love that snide cambot you—"

"One hundred thousand."

"Next to impossible."

"Then get Scoop to edit and—"

"Wait now."

Summer had been striding toward the door. "If you're not going to offer an extra 100,000 trubux then—"

"Well, I am prepared to offer that. One hundred thousand but no more than—"

"One hundred thousand'll be fine." He sat on the rubberoid sofa. "Now what about your suggested titles?"

"Apparently you really impressed Nugent's daughter."

"Meaning?"

"Merely that she told her father you were an excellent reporter. Nugent himself authorized me to go up to 100,000 for you on this."

"The titles?"

"This first one is, I'll admit right off, my own favorite. *Smashing the Zombium Racket*. How's that sound to you?"

"God-awful."

"Really? To me it's got snap and zing."

"It does. That's mainly why it's god-awful."

"How about *The Strange Case of Dr. Voodoo?* Sounds too much like a mystery show to me. Or there's *Zombium: Deadly Killer or latent Boon*?"

"We'll think up a title later." He rose. "Which edit room do I use?"

After searching through a stack of notes and memos, Taliaferro answered, "Room 23-A. You truly don't like *Smashing the Zombium Racket*?"

"Not much, no." He moved to the way out.

"Would you know anything about Palma's expenses out there?"

"Some."

"He claims you hired him as a backup man out there on Murdstone. He wants 37,000."

"Palma did work for me. Came near to saving my life

at one point. He's also the one who got us our first lead on Dr. Voodoo. His help was worth at least 37,000."

"I'll try to push it through. You wouldn't consider our paying him out of your bonus so—"

"I wouldn't."

"He also wants the money telepped to him out there on Murdstone care of something called Safari Tours, Ltd."

"That'll be his base of operations for a spell."

Taliaferro looked up. "Another romance?"

"Most of Palma's life is one romance or another."

"Oh, one more thing before you scoot." His editor had noticed a purple memo. "They wonder if it wouldn't play better if we could end our report with news of the current whereabouts of the Swain Brothers."

Summer said, "Nobody knows where they are."

"Then we'll have to keeping calling them the 'alleged drug-ring masterminds.' Is there some way you could maybe find—"

"I just dig up as much information as I can and report on it," he reminded. "I can't guarantee that I'll tie up all the loose ends or bring every single crook to justice. We did smash the Zombium racket. Or a big part of it anyway. You got almost three times as much time for the report as you expected. Settle for that."

"I'm more than satisfied." He dropped the purple memo. "I'll try to explain the situation to them."

"What's the deadline for a rough cut?"

"A week?"

"We'll try."

Taliaferro asked, "Aren't you a mite afraid the Swains will try to get even with you?"

"A mite." Summer left the office.

She was waiting for him in the gray corridor. "I wanted to talk with you, Jack."

After watching Vicky for a few seconds, Summer reached out and tapped her on the skull. "No, you're authentic."

"What did you think I was, an andy full of explosives?"

"My thoughts were on the Swains and their tricky ways."

"I'm really me."

"I appreciate that fact."

"Did you know I have my own private apartment on this Studio One satellite?"

He nodded. "I did, yes."

"Could you drop in for tea? There are a few things—"

"Sure."

Taking his arm, she walked him to an elevator. "First off, I wanted you to know I didn't force my father into authorizing that bonus for—"

The ebony elevator doors whispered open.

The fat human lady who was already in the cage gasped when she saw the two of them. "Victoria, you'll tear your reputation down by associating with this rogue."

"Hooey." They entered and the elevator started dropping.

"Summer," pleaded Henrietta Dorf, "leave this poor child alone and—"

"I'd like to Henrietta, but she's the boss's daughter. I fear I'll jeopardize my future with NewzNet unless I go along with her every—"

"I should've known better than to appeal to the decency of a man who has none."

The elevator reached Vicky's floor and opened.

"Nice of you to share your ride with me, Henrietta." Grinning, Summer followed Vicky out.

The living room was large and had opaque glaz walls. The floor was made up of several layers of rippled glaz.

"Where was I?" Vicky perched on the arm of a tin sofa. "Right, I was saying that I didn't have a darn thing to do with the bonus and all. What I mean is, I did tell my father I thought you did a terrific job out there and—"

"Vicky, hey," he told her, "I seldom get mad at anybody who gets extra money for me." From his pocket he took a bugsniffer.

"Why in the heck are you—"

"Just a hunch."

Ping!

There was a tiny spybug under the floating neowood coffee table.

"It's one of NewzNet's own." Summer threw it to the young woman.

"I think you're being very cheesy, father," she said into the bug before dropping it in a dispozhole.

"Better check out the other rooms."

"You do that," she said. "Especially my bedroom. Because that's where the rest of this conversation is going to lead us to."

Summer walked over to her. "I'll take care of that soon," he promised.